Surf
Ninjas

Surf
Ninjas

A NOVEL BY

A. L. Singer

BASED ON THE MOTION PICTURE
WRITTEN BY DAN GORDON

BANTAM BOOKS
NEW YORK · TORONTO · LONDON · SYDNEY · AUCKLAND

RL 5.6, age 10 and up
A Bantam Book / September 1993

ISBN 0–553–56361–0

Published simultaneously in the United States and Canada

PRINTED IN THE UNITED STATES OF AMERICA

RAD   10   9   8   7   6   5   4   3   2   1

A NEW LINE PRODUCTION
A film by NEAL ISRAEL
• SURF NINJAS •
ERNIE REYES, JR. • ROB SCHNEIDER
TONE LOC • JOHN KARLEN
and LESLIE NIELSEN as COLONEL CHI
Music Composed by DAVID KITAY
Production Designer MICHAEL NOVOTNY
Associate Producer ERNIE REYES, JR.
Written by DAN GORDON
Produced by EVZEN KOLAR
Directed by NEAL ISRAEL

Prologue

Johnny and Adam McQuinn were more than merely dudes. They were serious surf rats. Princes of the Pound Masters. Seekers of the Perfect Shred.

The surf was Numero Uno. Nothing else came close.

Well, except family. I mean, they were brothers. And they loved their dad, Mac—yes, the owner of Mac's Surfin' Turf, home of the most excellent shakes on Venice Beach. Oh, and Iggy. True, he was totally weird. Major airhead. A couple of sandwiches short of a picnic. But he was Johnny and Adam's best friend.

Later for that, though. When you got right down to it, surfing was top of the list. It was Johnny and Adam's reason for living. That alone would never change.

No way.

At least that was what they thought.

Then, one typical sunny morning, they had their first visit from the men in black. And from then on their lives were never quite the same.

Chapter 1

THERE WAS NO WARNING.

As far as the McQuinn brothers were concerned, this day was the same as all others. Breakfast, school, surfing. Outside, it was about as normal as you could get in Venice Beach, California. Blazing sun, killer waves, your standard muscle builders and weirdos on the beach. Johnny and Adam could see them all from their bungalow on the boardwalk.

But they couldn't see the Ninjas circling their house in broad daylight. And they couldn't see the old man with the patch over his eye, following close behind.

Had they known what was about to happen, they might have prepared. They might have dressed in martial arts gear, stashed some nunchucks and throwing stars in the kitchen.

Nunchucks? Throwing stars? *Well, maybe not. The truth: if you couldn't do it on a surfboard, Johnny and Adam knew nothing about it. What they really would have done was* split.

As it was, Johnny and Adam were dressed for the beach—Oakley sunglasses on Day-Glo straps, dive watches, and friendship wristbands. Adam munched on his cereal while furiously pressing buttons on a Game Gear. Johnny peered over his newspaper from across the table. "How can you eat that stuff?" he said with a sneer. "It's, like, ninety-five percent sugar and five percent corn."

Adam looked up from his Game Gear, which was covered with specks of milk. "Yeah, but if you hold your nose and put sugar on it, you can hardly taste the corn."

"Squank," Johnny said. "You're a surf rat, bro. You have to take care of the *temple*. Start the day with a little fruitage."

He grabbed a box of Froot Loops off the shelf and poured himself a bowlful.

Outside, the masked men peeked in a side window. They saw what they needed to see. Swiftly, in dead silence, they ran to the back of the house.

Johnny picked up the newspaper again, and Adam stifled a laugh. *Reading* was one of the last things his brother did.

Mac noticed, too, as he shuffled into the kitchen. "All of a sudden you have an interest in current events?"

Mac McQuinn had the build of someone who spent most of his life lifting things. His shoulders were almost as wide as the potbelly he lugged around. Years ago, when he had been a sailor, the belly hadn't been there. He had been lean and strong. And full of heart. He had adopted Johnny and Adam and raised them as a single parent. They didn't look a thing alike—Mac was Caucasian and his sons Asian—but that didn't stop the boys from calling him Dad. And it certainly didn't stop them from thinking he was the coolest over-thirty type around.

Johnny smiled. "Hey, check out the ladies' underwear ad, Dad!"

"Stylin'!" Adam said, craning his neck to see the paper.

"Guys?" Mac grabbed the newpaper away. "Homework?"

Johnny and Adam shot each other a look. Leave it to Dad to spoil a perfect morning.

"Dad," Johnny said, "I think we're falling into a rut. Every day it's the breakfast-homework fight. Can't we just go, 'We love each other,' and have a moment?"

"You're smooth, Johnny," Mac replied. "But you're not always going to get out of life's problems with this smooth stuff."

"I love you, Dad," Johnny said.

Mac was a sucker for those words—and Johnny knew it well. "I love you, too," he answered.

Sitting in the breakfast room, none of them could hear the back door open. None of them saw the hand reach into the kitchen drawer, pulling out the long-bladed knife.

"Guys," Mac went on, "every day when I get up to open the burger stand, you know what keeps me going? The thought that you're going to have it better than me. Which means you've got to do your homework. You can't live your whole lives surfing. You need something to fall back on."

"Way ahead of you, Dad," Adam said. "That's why we skateboard."

CRRASSH!

Mac jumped from the table. "What was that?"

"Probably the cat knocking something over," Johnny replied.

Adam frowned. "We have a cat?"

Mac went to the kitchen door. Glaring fiercely, he said, "I'd put down that knife if I were you."

Iggy sprang back from the counter. A few half-chopped chives lay on the cutting board in front of him—along with a dozen eggs, some cheese slices, and a loaf of bread.

"Seriously," Iggy said, "if you don't want chives in the omelet, I won't put them in."

Mac shook his head. "Iggy, you're here every morning. You're here every night. Don't your parents ever ask where you've been?"

"Mr. McQuinn, my parents are sealed in a biosphere in Arizona," Iggy said. "How about pimientos in the omelet?"

"*What?*" Mac said.

Johnny and Adam exchanged a knowing glance. Iggy was being . . . well, *Iggy*. The school psychologist had once told Iggy he had the most active "fantasy life" of any student he'd ever met. Translation: space cadet.

But you had to love the guy. At least Johnny and Adam thought so.

The men had heard the crash. They were on the roof now, and they froze. They would wait there. As long as necessary.

Iggy's face changed. His eyes brightened and got a far-off look at the same time. His mouth drew up into a half-smile. The "What-If Look," Johnny and Adam called it.

"What if," Iggy said, "they were shut off from the world in that big bubble thing in the desert? Totally top secret. Nobody allowed in or out. Just them and a lot of plants and animals and living things."

Mac stared at him, eyes wide and mouth open.

"It would be impossible to explain to a layman like you," Iggy said with a sigh.

Mac turned to his sons. "Why is he always making up these stories?"

"The school shrink says he has, like, delusions of grandeur and stuff," Johnny replied.

"But we think it's because he got creamed off his mountain bike in Hermosa," Adam said.

"Iggy," Mac pleaded, "why don't you try just telling the truth for once?"

"Okay, I guess I can trust you, Mr. McQuinn," Iggy said solemnly. "The truth is, my folks are astronauts. In fact, what if they were orbiting over the house any second?" He ran to the window and looked up. "Hey, Mom! Dad! Enjoy!"

The boy's voice was loud and near. But they were well out of sight. To a Ninja, invisibility is more than a skill. It is a way of life. Soon it would be time to act. Very soon.

Adam stuck his head out the window and shouted, "Don't land on the sun!"

Johnny jumped from his seat. "Yeow!" he shouted, lifting his feet as if he'd stepped on the sun.

Together, the three guys began dancing around on hot feet. A "First Three Dudes on the Sun" dance.

Mac shook his head. It was way too early for this. "Iggy," he said, looking at the clock, *"what if* you made that omelet in time for you guys to go to school?"

"Excellent idea," Iggy said. He raced into the kitchen, made the omelet, divided it in four, and threw each portion between slices of bread.

Mac sat at the table with a satisfied smile. The three boys grabbed their sandwiches and ran toward the front of the house. Adam made sure to take his Game Gear.

"Later, Dad!" Johnny called out, his mouth filled with egg.

Together they made tracks out the door.

It was time.

Above them, like tigers waiting for unsuspecting prey, the Ninjas leaped for the kill.

Chapter 2

"Uggghhhh . . . "

"*Ohhhhhhh!*"

The sounds of pain were short and sudden. But Johnny, Adam, and Iggy never heard those sounds. They were too busy trying to out-burp each other.

Behind them, the two Ninjas crumpled to the lawn.

The old man stood over them. He had thrown off his disguise. Underneath he was trim, well muscled, and clad in black. He glared at his victims through his one active eye. His body was still in a *kamae*, a fighting stance. As a Ninja, he knew to remain ready for any counterattack.

But from the looks of the two men on the lawn, he would have nothing to worry about.

"*BRRRRRRRRRRRRUPPP!*"

Iggy's belch was the best yet. Johnny and Adam looked at each other with wide grins. "Tips, nips, and rips!" they shouted at the same time.

They touched fingertips. They crashed their

chests together. Then they burped together. Tips, nips, and rips. A time-honored tradition.

"I have a feeling today's going to be a great day," Johnny said. "Epic."

"Crunching," Iggy said.

"Tasty," Adam piped up.

They crossed the street to Iggy's car. They never thought to look behind. They never saw the three men.

Minutes later, Iggy pulled into the high school parking lot. The place was jumping. Rollerbladers circled around them. Kids played Hacky Sack on the lawn. Music blared from car speakers all over.

As he got out, Iggy pulled a Frisbee from under his seat. He and the McQuinn brothers began tossing it around.

"What if," Iggy said, "like, last night the little homework fairies snuck into my house and did my homework and so when I open up my bag, it's right here?" He opened his bag, looked inside, and shook his head. "I hate those guys. They never do my homework, but they always drink the milk I put out for them."

Adam's eyes widened. "Really?"

"Rank!" Iggy shot back.

"I need a homework alibi," Johnny said. "I could tell them I was hammered by the fact I found out I was adopted last night."

"You were adopted last night?" Iggy replied.

"Why didn't your dad just adopt you when you were a baby?"

"We *were* adopted when we were babies," Johnny said.

But Iggy already had that *look*. "What if *I'm* adopted? And my real old man was really a rich king and stuff?"

Adam rolled his eyes. "Yeah, kings are always putting up their kids for adoption."

"But if my dad were a king, he wouldn't care about homework," Iggy said, "and if the teacher ragged on me he could, like, buy the school and fire them or, like, put them in dungeons, you know? Crispy, huh? Enjoy!"

They turned the corner to the front of the school. On the marquee above the entrance there was a message in huge letters:

SURF VIEW JUNIOR AND SENIOR HIGH SCHOOL
WELCOMES THE BABA-RAM OF MEE GROB

A Cadillac limo pulled up to the front, surrounded by motorcycle cops and followed by three unmarked cars. From the antenna of the limo flew a flag Johnny and Adam had never seen before. On the school roof, a SWAT team clutched M-16s, looking at the crowd below.

"Whoa," Adam said, "what's this all about?"

Johnny slapped his head. "I'm in trouble. I was supposed to do the welcoming speech for this visiting guru guy in front of the assembly second period."

"Squank," Iggy said. "Have you figured out what you're going to say to this Baba-Ram guy?"

"Nay. But now I also need a Baba-Ram alibi."

"I know!" Iggy piped up. "Tell them you just found out you were adopted!"

"Good, Iggs," Adam said. But his eyes were on a cute girl who was approaching them.

They smiled at each other as they stepped into the driveway from opposite sides.

"Hey, Adam," the girl said with a dazzling smile.

"You know, Betty," Adam said, "if I were going to build a condo, I'd put it here because the view is so sweet."

The girl blushed. Her smile grew wider, her eyes warmer.

"Where does he come up with this stuff?" Johnny muttered to Iggy.

HONNNNNNKK!

Johnny, Adam, and Iggy jumped onto the sidewalk. An enormous garbage truck skidded up the driveway, barely missing them. It came to a stop, leaving long rubber tracks.

"Hey, you kids! Watch where you're going!" shouted a policeman beside the truck.

Kids? No *kids* could have jumped away from that truck. It took skill, years of experience on a surfboard, dodging and weaving. Three ordinary *kids* would have been Fruit Roll-ups by then.

But try explaining that to a flatfoot.

Shaking themselves off, the three guys walked to the school.

And the two men in the garbage truck

watched—through dark Asian eyes, and without a trace of remorse.

The policeman waved them onward, and they drove into the parking lot. By that time the area was clear, except for a few latecomers. The two men got out and ran to the back of the truck. When the lot was completely empty of people, they pulled the lever.

The truck's immense rear section gaped open. But there were no clumps of rotten food inside, no mounds of twisted metal or crushed cardboard boxes.

Instead, ten masked Ninjas scampered out. In silence, led by the two drivers, they scaled the wall of the school. When they got to the top, they were in position. Behind the backs of the unsuspecting SWAT team.

They moved in for the attack. This time, there would be no mistakes.

Chapter 3

$\mathcal{J}$T WASN'T EASY, but Johnny kept his cool. The auditorium was full. He was standing on the stage in front of a thousand kids. The principal, Mr. Dutton, was having a cow at him. To Johnny's left the entire high school chorus milled around onstage. To his right, the old dude with the flowing beard and robe sat front and center in the audience. Around the Baba-Ram was a bunch of slightly younger flowing-beard-and-robe types.

"Let me put this in your language, dude." Mr. Dutton's head kind of bounced to the right and left. He slouched a little forward and bent his knees. Johnny had seen this action before. Mr. Dutton was trying to be "hip." He looked ridiculous.

"This may be a very groovy scene for you," Mr. Dutton went on, pronouncing his words carefully, "but I take it pretty seriously. You got it, Daddy-O? In other words, don't blow it. You prepared?"

"Everything's under control, sir," Johnny replied.

"Something that has to do with traditional Eastern ceremony, right? You researched it? Like you promised?"

"Hey . . . of course."

As Mr. Dutton walked away, Johnny looked at the old guru, or whatever he was. *Baba-Ram, huh?* he thought.

"I need some people," Johnny mumbled to himself.

He ran into the chorus. There had to be three or four dudes who would help him out.

Soon Mr. Dutton strolled up to the podium. He tapped the mike, then began the program: "I am pleased to welcome one of the world's greatest spiritual leaders, the Most Revered and Esteemed, His Eminence, the Baba-Ram of Mee Grob. Johnny McQuinn has prepared a welcoming presentation in what I have been assured is authentic ethnic style."

He looked up to the heavens. It hadn't been easy getting the Baba-Ram to come. The last thing he needed was for Johnny to start a cultural war between the two countries.

The house lights went down. Slowly the curtains opened. From deep upstage, Johnny began walking forward with three chorus boys. Dressed in choral robes, they began a solemn chant: "Baaaaaaaa . . . Baaaaaaaa . . . Baaaaaaaa . . . "

Mr. Dutton's face lit up. He sighed with relief.

Then Johnny's group got to the front of the stage. Their hips started moving. On a signal from Johnny, they sang to the Beach Boys tune "Barbara Ann":

Ba-ba-ba . . . Ba-ba-ba-Ram
Ba-ba-ba . . . Ba-ba-ba-Ram
Baba-Ram, take my hand,
Baba-Ram.
You got me rocking and a-rollin',
Rockin' and a-reelin', Baba-Ram . . .

The audience rose to its feet, screaming and singing.

As for Mr. Dutton, well, he was taking second place in the Surf View Gaping Contest.

First place belonged to the Baba-Ram.

The junior high was to see the Baba-Ram at a later assembly. Which meant Adam had to sit through geography.

Mrs. Robertson was on a quest. She was determined to take a dry subject and wring all the juice out of it. As she pulled down an unlabeled world map, she turned to Adam.

"Adam, would you step up to the map and show us the location of Spain?"

Adam got up. As he walked to the front, he stared solemnly at the map. "You mean, *the* Spain?"

"You should know this from your homework last night," Mrs. Robertson snapped.

"Oh!" Adam smiled. "The *homework* Spain!"

He pointed to a big lump of land in the lower left part of the map. "Some people think Spain is here."

The smart kids laughed. Time for another try.

"On the other hand, there is a school of thought that claims Spain is here." He pointed to the very bottom of the map. More laughter. "Those people, too, are mistaken. So where is Spain? It could be here. . . ."

Adam rambled on, too preoccupied to see the black-masked face looking upside down through the window.

The Ninja had found his target. Leaning over the roof, he braced himself. Swiftly he pulled out a throwing star. He drew his arm back, ready to hurl it through the window. Ready to slice little Adam McQuinn in front of his class.

"Urggghh!"

Adam's assassin gasped for breath. His arm froze. Someone yanked him back up to the roof with a wicked choke hold. He tried to struggle, but it was impossible.

The last thing he saw before blacking out was the face of his attacker. The face of the man with the eye patch.

Screeeek!

The roof door creaked halfway open. The patch-eyed man did not even look. He knew he had to disappear. He laid the Ninja on the roof, right next to the unconscious SWAT team man. Then, as silently as he had struck, the patch-eyed man climbed down the building's side.

Screeeek! Out of the old door stepped two men. One of them was a detective, a tall African American with a weary look in his eye. Spence was his name. Lieutenant Robert C. Spence of the L.A. Police Department. The other man was a uniformed police sergeant, a beefy white guy named Bork.

They looked at the two unconscious figures sprawled on the rooftop.

Sergeant Bork squatted next to the SWAT team member. "Looks like Mr. Black Pajamas got Henderson from behind."

"Yeah," answered Lieutenant Spence, "but then who got Mr. Black Pajamas?"

Spence thought about it for a minute. Something was going on here, something not so simple. And like it or not, he was in the middle of it.

"Why does this stuff always happen the day I'm supposed to go on vacation?" he muttered. He pulled a walkie-talkie from his jacket and barked into it: "I want you to seal off the entire area and get the guru out of here!"

In the classroom below them, unaware of what had happened, Adam rambled on: "Since the dawn of man, Spain has appeared in many places, confounding explorers and mapmakers throughout the ages—"

"*Attention, students,*" blared Mr. Dutton's voice over the loudspeaker. "*Due to security concerns, we will be evacuating the entire school. Classes are therefore suspended for the rest of the day.*"

"Yeaaaahhhhh!" The cheer went up in each classroom, practically rocking the building.

Adam smiled. He was off the hook. Later for Spain.

He walked out of the classroom and found Iggy and Johnny out front. Together they watched the police rushing Baba-Ram and his group into the limo.

Then they headed for the car—and the beach.

On their way, a pair of dark eyes watched them from the driver's side of the garbage truck. The driver was alone now. His partner was lying on the roof of the school. But his mission was not over. Oh, no. It had just begun.

A half hour later, Johnny and Adam were riding the waves. Unfortunately, so was everyone else in school. Except Iggy. He was off waxing his surfboard—which he seemed to do an awful lot.

Johnny paddled up to his younger brother. The two of them rocked up and down, keeping an eye out for the next wave. "Drab," Johnny said, "did you catch my off-the-lip rail grab? I was going Richter till that Val dropped in."

Adam shook his head. "He's an aqua booter. His disco maneuvers are going to get his face planted."

" 'Tsup, Adam!" a junior high girl called out as she paddled by.

"Hello, darling," Adam replied. "I love that color on you."

Her smile made the sun look like a minor glare.

Johnny looked at Adam in awe. "How do you do it?"

Behind them, out of sight, a surfer paddled up from the shore. He was dressed in black from head to toe. His garbage truck was parked right near the beach. And he held a spear gun in his right hand.

He grinned. This was the perfect setup. The boys were alone. Old Patch-Eye, their savior, was nowhere to be seen.

The Ninja lined the boys up in his sights. They were rising out of the water and onto their boards—even better! Now they were bigger targets.

He felt himself sinking. He clutched his board, trying to keep aim. The boys were turning toward him now. They were rising. On top of a wave . . . cresting . . .

The Ninja tried to swim away. The wave was enormous. Johnny's surfboard was coming closer, right toward his head.

Wipeout. The Ninja had heard the word. He knew surfers feared it. He knew that to be creamed by a wave was a hurtful experience.

And no amount of Ninjutsu could protect you from that.

Thinking quickly, the Ninja did what he knew he had to do. He dropped his spear gun and screamed.

Under the roar of the wave, Johnny heard nothing. But he did feel his board bump against something hard. Struggling to keep his balance, he rode in to shore.

After some high fives, low fives, and in-between fives, he and Adam headed up the beach. That was when Johnny noticed the dent in the front of his board.

"Whoa," he said, "I think I fully dinged my board on a rock or something."

He looked up to see Iggy approaching with his

newly waxed surfboard. "Hey, bro," Johnny called out, "we're leaving."

"Now?" Iggy's shoulders sank with disappointment. "Squank. I had some moves in me, too."

Johnny whispered the sad truth into his brother's ear. "He's never surfed a day in his life."

"I'm aware," Adam whispered back.

"Hey," Iggy said, "tomorrow we'll start early, okay?"

Iggy bounced along with them, back to the McQuinn house. His board shone in the sunlight, as untouched as the day he'd bought it.

Moments later, in a secluded corner of the beach, a man washed up on the shore. A man dressed in black and barely breathing.

Johnny and Adam did not know how lucky they were.

Chapter 4

DEEP IN THE MISTS of the South China Sea, thirteen thousand miles from California, stands the island of Patu San. It rises from the water, a mountain of rocky crags and lush forests. At its base is a small village. Its people are peaceful and steeped in an ancient, slow-moving life.

But through most of the day a shadow is cast over the village. High above Patu San, shrouded by a fog that never lifts, stands the Fortress of Sri Wan. It was built, rock by rock, to be the strongest building in the Eastern Hemisphere. Through centuries of warfare, against the ablest soldiers, Sri Wan was never penetrated.

Until the uprising of Colonel Chi.

Fierce and cold-hearted, Chi took over Patu San from its wise spiritual leaders. He created a cruel dictatorship. Political enemies and shoplifters were treated with equal dispatch.

All were brought to Colonel Chi's headquarters, the high-tech Dungeon of Sri Wan.

Chi lived in that dungeon. To him, there was no

sweeter sound than the screaming of tortured humanity. Chi was no stranger to pain himself. Half his face and his entire right hand had been destroyed in the Great Uprising. Over his mutilated half-face, he wore a hideous bronze mask with a hinged jaw. And on his right hand was his infamous and fearsome tiger claw. The claw was real, and Chi operated it electronically via a battery pack on his chest. Legend had it that Chi had defeated the tiger with his bare hands. (There were no eyewitnesses, however.)

Colonel Chi was in the dungeon on the day Johnny and Adam narrowly missed being killed by Ninjas. In Sri Wan, it was business as usual. Prisoners groaned, bone-thin, manacled to the stone wall. Others lay stretched out on racks, grimacing and screaming for forgiveness. Still others awaited torture by whipping, by hot pincers, and by boiling oil. Escape was impossible, for the dungeon was surrounded by a moat stocked with crocodiles and man-eating fish.

It was, Chi liked to say, a creative setup.

Chi approached one of his captives. Barechested and strapped to a whipping post, the man shook with fear. "You will talk," Chi snarled. "I promise you."

Manchu, the Executioner of Sri Wan, looked at his commander with expectant eyes. No one in Patu San was as large as Manchu, or as hideous. Just looking at his face was torture enough for any mortal, but Manchu made it worse. He had an appetite for inflicting bodily harm.

"Manchu," Colonel Chi grumbled to his assistant, "give him pain."

Manchu's lips twisted upward into a grotesque version of a smile. "Pain," he said. "Yes!"

He ambled over to a computer keyboard and punched in some coordinates. On a spring-loaded lever, a cat-o'-nine-tails began lashing the prisoner.

Bleeeeeeeep!

Chi's phone began to ring. He reached for it with his electronic claw. The claw grabbed the end of a torture rack.

Bleeeeeeeep!

He tried again. The claw swept across the table, knocking over a soda can and missing the phone.

Bleeeeeeeep!

Roaring with frustration, Chi tried again. The claw finally did what he wanted. "Hello!" he barked into the receiver. "Are they dead? . . . I don't want to hear excuses! The two boys will die tonight or you will answer to me here in the Dungeon of Sri Wan!"

With that, he slammed down the phone and stormed away.

In a dark corner of the dungeon, out of Colonel Chi's earshot, two emaciated prisoners stood chained to the wall. The first one turned his face toward the other. He opened his parched mouth to speak. Though his voice was no more than a rasp, there was a tiny note of hope: "They are not dead!"

The second prisoner's eyes glimmered for the first time in months. "The legends are true," he whispered, the joyous words choking in his throat. "The boys are alive!"

Chapter 5

IGGY WAS THE FIRST to meet the patch-eyed man. Coming out of a store along the boardwalk, Iggy walked into him.

The man stared down at Iggy, his eye like a hundred-watt lantern. The crags on his face were like chisel marks, and he seemed to look right through Iggy.

Iggy's mouth dropped. He wanted to scream, but no sound came out. A minute ago he'd been walking safely down the boardwalk with Johnny and Adam. Now he wished he hadn't ducked into the store. Helplessly he looked behind him, hoping for some eyewitnesses.

When he turned around, the patch-eyed man was gone.

He sprinted up to Johnny and Adam. "Hey, you guys?" he said breathlessly. "Do you ever think you're being followed by this real freaky-looking guy with this patch over his eye and this real scary-looking scar?"

Johnny looked at him blankly. "No."

"I feel like that all the time, but now I think it's happening for real!"

The three of them turned around and looked. Nothing unusual was going on.

"You must have been hammered by too many waves," Johnny said.

He shot a wink at Adam, who picked up the hint. "Yeah, that's got to be it."

The sun was setting as they walked into Mac's Surfin' Turf. There they grabbed a few burgers and hung out by the prep table till closing time.

Mac raced around the kitchen, cleaning up and preparing for the next day. "So," he said, "how was school today?"

"I was this close to finding Spain when we all had to leave early," Adam said. "Now I'll never know where it is."

Johnny nodded. "They tried to make *me* find Spain once. I said it could be anywhere."

"So did I!" Adam said with a grin.

"All right, bro! Tips, nips, and rips!"

Mac sighed wearily. "Take out the trash, okay, guys?"

Johnny and Adam lugged the trash can to the back of the kitchen. They pushed the door open and hoisted the can into the dark alley behind the restaurant.

But they only got two steps. Standing before them was the patch-eyed man.

The can made a dull thud as it dropped to the ground. Johnny and Adam backed slowly into the kitchen. "D-Dad . . . ?" Johnny squeaked.

Mac stared at them, dumbfounded. "What's wrong with you two?"

"Remember that guy you said would show up if we didn't eat our vegetables?" Adam said. "He's here!"

"Hey, Adam," Johnny warned, "that's not the bogeyman, that's a homicidal killer."

Slowly the man came into the light. He stood at the threshold of the kitchen, staring straight at Mac.

"Oh, right," Iggy blurted. "When *I* see him I'm crazy—but when *you* see him, he's a homicidal killer."

Iggy's words hung in the air, unanswered. Johnny and Adam stared at their dad. Mac was silent, gazing at the patch-eyed man as if at a ghost returning from the dead.

When the man spoke, his voice was deep and gravelly: "Hello, Mac."

CRRRASSSSHHHH!

In a shower of glass, the windows burst in from all sides. Eight Ninjas leaped into the kitchen.

The patch-eyed man grabbed Johnny and Adam and pushed them behind him. Then, like a wild animal protecting its young, he turned to face the attackers.

They faced off. Silent. Tensed. Eight against one. Who would make the first move?

The eight soon became seven. One of the Ninjas spotted Iggy, standing unprotected. While all other eyes were concentrated on the patch-eyed man, the sixth Ninja slowly backed Iggy up to the prep table.

Iggy gulped. "So, what if, for the sake of argument, you've already hit me and I'm down like this—"

He grunted and doubled over as if he were hit, then fell under the prep table. "Am I out of the way now?" he called out. "Would you like me somewhere else or can we say this is cool?"

"*YYYEEEEEEEAAAAAAAAAGGGGGGGHHHHH!*"

The roar was human, but barely. The prep table began to tip. Iggy looked up in shock.

It was Mac. His arm muscles bulging, his teeth gritted, he pushed the table on its side and lifted it.

The battle was on.

Like a knight with a two-hundred-pound shield, Mac charged into the Ninjas. Some jumped out of the way, but two were pinned helplessly to the order counter.

Another Ninja caught Mac by surprise. With the stealth and power of a black belt, the Ninja whacked Mac on the shoulder.

It was enough to destroy an ordinary human. But Mac turned, clutched the Ninja in a bear hug, and threw him onto the grill.

Tsssssss . . .

As the Ninja's scream resounded, Mac grabbed another Ninja and jammed his face into the cotton candy machine.

One by one, the other Ninjas attacked the patch-eyed man. They whirled at him, legs and arms thrusting. Coolly, with razorlike precision, the man fought back. He wasted no motion, hardly let out a grunt of effort.

Johnny and Adam crouched low. They appreciated the stranger's effort, but it was time to make tracks. Their skateboards were nearby, and they would have to do.

Frantically they stepped on the boards and maneuvered their way through the kitchen. They ducked as a black-clad body flew over their heads, landing in a heap near Iggy.

"Enjoy!" Iggy called to the Ninja.

Johnny and Adam lurched left and right. The back door was only a few feet away . . .

Sssssssssshhhiick!

A throwing star sliced through the air. Its hooks caught Johnny's and Adam's sleeves, pinning them to the wall.

The skateboards went flying away. Johnny and Adam were prisoners in their dad's restaurant. And a leering martial arts nut was heading right toward them.

"Aaaaaaaagh!" they screamed.

Mac heard—and saw. With a burst of strength, he lifted a wooden bench and smashed it into the Ninja who had pinned his sons.

The Ninja fell to the ground. Mac whirled around, fighting off more of them. They seemed to be emerging from the walls.

The patch-eyed man ran to Johnny and Adam. He pulled the throwing star out of the wall, then turned toward Mac.

Mac was fending off the rest of the attackers with a meat cleaver. "Zatch!" he screamed. "Get the boys out of here!"

Johnny and Adam looked on in disbelief. Their dad seemed to *know* this guy.

Zatch, the patch-eyed man, turned to the brothers. "Come quickly!" he commanded.

"We're not leaving our dad!" Johnny replied.

Iggy hopped up and joined them. "Normally I'd stay and fight to the death, too, but it *is* a school night."

With that, Iggy raced out the door. And before Johnny or Adam could say a thing, Zatch was dragging them out by the collars of their shirts.

And Zatch was strong.

Chapter 6

IN THE COOL SAND their footsteps were silent. There was no moon, so the beach was pitch black. No one saw Zatch force Johnny and Adam along the beach toward the piers.

Behind them, afraid to be left alone, was Iggy.

When they were under the pilings, Zatch pushed all three of them into a remote corner.

"I wanted you to know," Iggy said, "I really felt safe in your arms, and I've never said that to a man before."

But Johnny was furious. "What are you doing?" he snapped. "You can't leave our dad all alone with those guys. Get your hands off me!"

"Quiet!"

It was only one word, and it was hardly more than a whisper. But Johnny, Adam, and Iggy all fell silent. When Zatch spoke, you listened.

" . . . Your Highnesses," Zatch said, finishing his sentence. "You must be quiet."

"Who were those quimbies in the camouflage pajamas?" Adam demanded.

"Boy," Iggy said, "those uniforms really give them the chameleonlike ability to blend in with their surroundings—hey, watch out! There's one now!" He bent down and picked up a strand of seaweed. "Oh. False alarm."

Johnny glared at the other two. "Will you guys just be quiet and let him—" He turned to Zatch, but no one was there.

"Where'd he go?" Johnny's voice echoed among the pilings, then died in the dark stillness.

"I don't know," Iggy answered, "but I miss him."

"Didn't you guys hear what he said?" Johnny exclaimed. "He called us *Your Highnesses*!"

"The guy is a nut case," Adam said. "Let's go back and find Dad."

They ran back to Mac's Surfin' Turf—or what was left of it. All the windows had been smashed. The dining room was a tangle of overturned chairs and tables. The kitchen looked as if it had been run through a giant Cuisinart.

No Ninjas were in sight. Neither was Mac.

"They have taken him."

Johnny, Adam, and Iggy spun around at the sound of Zatch's voice. There he was, standing in a corner as if he'd just materialized.

"Whoa," Adam said. "How does he do that?"

Johnny stepped toward Zatch. "Who took him?"

Zatch seemed to soften at Johnny's forcefulness. "The same ones who want you dead, Your Highness."

"Why do you keep calling us that?" Johnny demanded.

"Because you are crown princes and your father was a king."

"Whoa, it's true!" Iggy shouted. "I'm not dreaming, am I? Remember when I said 'What if my father was a king?' This is completely insane. I'm a crown prince!"

"Not you," Zatch said. "*They* are crown princes and *their* father was a king."

"And *you* are a maniac," Johnny shot back at Zatch, "and your father was a maniac!"

"And *his* father was a maniac," Adam chimed in, "and his father—"

"Adam, don't help me," Johnny said.

The brothers turned angrily from Zatch and walked away.

Iggy smiled at Zatch. "Good thinking, O Patched One. Let them think they're really crown princes. We'll use them for decoys." He called over his shoulder to Johnny and Adam, "I'll handle the cops, guys. I know their direct line!" Then he winked at Zatch and said softly, "This could be extremely dangerous, so I want you to keep one eye on my *amigos* and one . . . well, do the best you can."

As Iggy ran out the back door, Zatch called to Johnny and Adam, "We need to talk."

The brothers turned around, uncertain of what to do next. Zatch gestured toward the open door.

The three of them stepped onto the boardwalk. A lazy saltwater breeze blew against them as they walked. "Search your memories, Your Highnesses,"

Zatch pleaded. "What do you remember of your life before you came to America?"

"What do you mean *before*? We were born here," Adam protested. He turned to Johnny. "Weren't we?"

Johnny looked at his brother, then dropped his eyes. He couldn't answer yes, but he couldn't answer no. There was much about his youth he had blocked out of his mind. The years before Mac. He had distant images, yes—but the people and places were so strange, so . . . so *foreign*.

Zatch could see the memories playing across Johnny's face. "Your brother was too young to remember," he said. "But you must remember something of Patu San."

"*Patu San . . .*" Johnny repeated. Why was that name familiar? "Patu San . . ."

"Porta-San?" Adam piped up. "Those toilets at the construction sites? Hey, I give up the throne."

"No, not Porta-San," Zatch snapped. "Patu San! For four thousand years, Patu San was ruled by one line of warrior kings. It was the most peaceful place on earth. But in the Time of the Ancients, it was foretold that in the seventh cycle after men flew as eagles to the moon—"

"Wow, you completely lost me already," Adam said.

"—the peace would be broken by bloodshed," Zatch went on, "and the Time of the Tiger would begin. A violent coup, led by Colonel Chi, a foreign mercenary, devastated our country. As head of the Imperial Guard, I was entrusted to protect the Royal

Princes, Yow-ni and Ad-Ham, from Chi's determination to kill them. They were just children at the time."

"Why would Chi want to kill them?" Johnny asked.

"The prophecies foretold that Yow-ni would grow to be a great warrior, and Ad-Ham a great seer—and that on Yow-ni's sixteenth birthday he would ascend to the throne, and Patu San would be free once more."

"I'm going to be sixteen in two weeks," Johnny said.

"I know, Your Highness." Zatch nodded sagely. "As I carried the young princes away from the palace, I fought off Colonel Chi, who fell under a stampeding elephant. I understand he sustained disfiguring injuries. Nonetheless, as the prophecies foretold, the entire royal family was killed—except the two young crown princes, who escaped."

"Wow, that was a really excellent story," Adam said.

"But what about Mac?" Johnny asked. "How does he fit in?"

Zatch walked onto the sand and sat down. As Johnny and Adam joined him, they spotted Iggy in a phone booth by a darkened shop.

"Mac was a former American sailor," Zatch began. "He had worked for the royal family for many years. His loyalty to them was beyond reproach. It was into his arms that I entrusted the two children. You were those children, Your Highnesses. For Colonel Chi you are the living threat to his rule. To me you are the living prophecy who will free our country."

"Don't you have to drive to do that?" Adam asked. "I'd *really* like to drive."

"Look," Johnny insisted, "we don't want to free anything. We just want our dad back!"

"Mac is inconsequential," Zatch said. "We are all inconsequential. The rebellion is what counts now. You must return with me to Patu San."

"*Our dad is not inconsequential!*" Johnny shot back. "He is, like, super-consequential, okay?"

"Right," Adam added. "He's turbo-consequential. He's mega-consequential—"

"Adam, don't help me!" Johnny said. He turned back to Zatch. "*You* are inconsequential. Your prophecy is inconsequential and your rebellion is inconsequential."

"You have no sense of duty or honor," Zatch replied.

"Hey, *you* have no sense of humor, okay?" Adam said.

"Listen, *amigo*. We're going to the *federales, comprende*?" Johnny turned toward the phone booth. "Later."

"I do not need to convince you," Zatch said calmly. "It is not something you must choose or not choose. It is your destiny. It has chosen you."

Iggy slammed the phone down and began walking toward them. "Seriously, I got it all wired," he called out. "Chino said to meet Tony and Riff at Doc's drugstore. The shipment moves tonight."

Adam rolled his eyes. He recognized the lines from *West Side Story.*

But Johnny just stared at him, bewildered. "Shipment?"

"Rank," Iggy said. "I called the cops and they said to meet us at your dad's burger place. That is, if it's cool with our sight-challenged friend."

They turned—and Zatch was gone again.

"Hey, he disappeared!" Adam said.

"Yeah," Johnny replied, "and all he left behind is a tiny little pot of gold."

Iggy's eyes widened. "Really?"

"Rank back," Johnny replied.

"Come on," Adam said. "Let's blow."

They could see flashing lights before they could make out Mac's Surfin' Turf. As they neared it, they realized the police had already been there. The place was cordoned off with yellow police tape.

Iggy stopped. "Guys, let's not go into this without a plan."

"A plan?" Johnny asked warily.

"Listen," Iggy said, "if they find out you're going to be living without any 'rents, they'll stick you in protective services—which is even worse than my latchkey number, living at home with Lupe, the maid from hell."

"So what do we do?" Adam asked.

"Just say you have an uncle staying with you," Iggy said.

"We don't have an uncle," Johnny replied.

"You do now," Iggy said with a sly grin.

"You?" Johnny exhaled with annoyance. "They're never going to buy you're our uncle. Forget it!"

"Okay, I was hoping I wouldn't have to play this card." Iggy sighed. "I'm going to have to *command* you to do this."

"*Command* us?" Johnny looked at him as if Iggy had finally lost his mind.

"Seriously, you guys are the *decoys*," Iggy insisted. "I'm the real king, so you have to do as I command, because you know too much. And if you betray me, I'll have to kill you. Okay?"

"Oh," Johnny said. "That's reasonable."

"Totally fair," Adam agreed.

They began walking again toward the Surfin' Turf—ready to begin Operation Uncle Iggy.

Chapter 7

"**A**RE YOU GUYS OPEN?" The surf dude poked his head into the smashed, hollowed-out remains of Mac's Surfin' Turf.

His voice floated over the upturned tables and broken chairs of the dining room. There was no answer, but he could see people in the kitchen. "Are you open?" he called out, more loudly.

Johnny McQuinn didn't hear a word. He was in the kitchen with Adam and Lieutenant Spence, explaining the story of Patu San. Spence busily took notes. Around them, Sergeant Bork and his men looked for clues.

" . . . and so," Johnny said, "it was into the arms of Mac, a former American sailor, that we were entrusted as we left Patu San forever."

Spence put down his clipboard. "Man, that is the longest story I have ever heard."

"Tell me about it," Adam said. "I've heard it twice."

Arms behind his back, Lieutenant Spence began ambling into the dining room. "So," he said, "you want me to buy that that Colonel Cheese sent these eastly camo Ninjas here because he's ballistic about your old man?"

"All we know," Johnny said, "is that these sketchy, cheese-footed Ninjas dropped our pop and went oh-double-haywire on the food hut!"

"Uh, forgive me for speaking English," Sergeant Bork interrupted, walking into the kitchen, "but I think I found something." He held out a dagger. "It's just like the ones we found over at the school, where they tried to assassinate the Baba-Ram guy."

As Spence took the dagger, Bork pulled him aside. "Captain just called," he mumbled into Spence's ear. "You can kiss Tahoe good-bye. He wants you on this thing till it's over."

"This is the third cancel they've made on me this year!" Spence complained.

"Sorry, man."

"My girl, Charlene, isn't going to like this. If she shoots me, tell the department I want you to have my benefits." With a sigh, Spence turned back to Johnny and Adam. "All right, boys, let me drive you back to your digs. And I want to hear the whole deal again. This time, the Classic Comic version."

They walked toward the front door. The two surfers perked up. "Excuse me," the first one said to Spence. "Are you open yet? Can I get a shake?" With a grin, he turned to his friend. "Trust me, it's worth the wait. Killer shakes."

"Go away," Spence grumbled. "Can't you see we're renovating?"

He led Johnny and Adam outside and into his

unmarked sedan. They drove to the McQuinn house, followed by an L.A.P.D. black-and-white. As they pulled up in front of the house, Spence asked, "You sure you guys are cool tonight?"

"Yeah, we told you," Johnny said. "Our uncle is crashing with us."

Spence glanced at the notes on his clipboard. "Oh, that's right. Your uncle . . . Iggy. I'm going to leave a patrol unit outside your house tonight just in case anybody tries to mess with you. But you know what I think?"

"What?" Adam asked.

"I think some guys were probably leaning on your old man, so they came in and broke the place up. Your dad probably split. He's chilling out someplace and he'll probably be back tonight. Don't worry."

"My dad isn't *chilling* someplace," Johnny retorted. "He loves us. He wouldn't ever split on us."

Spence's gruffness disappeared. He looked at Johnny and nodded gently. "Yeah. I . . . I guess you're right, kid."

From the front of the house, a shaft of amber light spilled across the lawn. Spence looked up to see a potbellied man with a baseball cap standing in the open front door. He was glad the boys' uncle was home.

"Come on, boys!" the man called out. "Time to get in here and clean up your room, or no boob tube tonight. And I know best because, as you know, I'm thirty-seven."

Spence's eyes narrowed suspiciously.

41

"Uncle Iggy's very proud of his age," Johnny said. "No one thought he'd make it this far."

"Okay, get out of here," Spence replied.

As Johnny and Adam ran into the house, Spence got out and walked over to the patrol car. "You two keep your eyes open tonight," he said, leaning into the front window. "I don't want anything coming down on those kids."

A buzz from the car radio interrupted Spence. The driver answered it, then held it out. "It's for you, Lieutenant."

Spence took a deep breath and grabbed the receiver. "Charlene," he said softly. "I—I know, baby, but . . . but . . . but . . . You can't go to Tahoe without me. Charlene? Hello?"

Slumping sadly, he handed the receiver back to the policeman. "I need a life."

Inside the McQuinn living room, Johnny and Adam plopped on the couch. Neither of them said a word. Without Mac, the house didn't feel right.

Iggy yanked the pillow out from under his shirt. "Did you see me give that cop the royal rank? He fully bought it."

"Yeah, yeah," Johnny said distractedly. "You were great."

"Did you notice how I worked my age in there?" Iggy went on.

"*That's* what sold it," Adam remarked.

Iggy picked up on his friends' mood. He sat down and shut up. From the squad car outside, a low rumble of conversation filtered in through the open front window.

"Bro?" Adam finally said.

"Yeah, bro?" Johnny replied.

"I'm feeling a little . . . you know, scared."

"Don't worry. I'm here. We'll be okay." Johnny took his brother's hand.

They began thumb-wrestling. For the first time since they'd stepped inside, smiles broke across their faces. "Pin!" Johnny called out, trapping his brother's thumb.

"Johnny," Adam said, "what if that Zatch guy was telling the truth? What if it *is* my destiny to be a prince and a seer, and it's, like, your destiny to be a prince and a warrior?"

"And don't forget," Iggy reminded them, "I'm the king."

"Iggy, you *can't* be the king of Patu San," Johnny said. "You're not Asian."

Iggy gave him a smug grin. "I've got two words for you: David Carradine in *Kung Fu*."

Adam was in no mood for Iggy's delusions. He grabbed his Game Gear and flicked it on. A logo materialized on the screen—a strange yin/yang symbol, with a two-headed dragon looming over the top. Under the symbol were the words SURF NINJAS.

"That's weird," Adam said. "Where's Shinobi? I thought I was playing Shinobi."

He pressed PLAY. The logo dissolved and a boy appeared. Adam smiled. The guy looked a lot like him.

The boy put on a headband, which showed

the yin/yang-and-dragon symbol. Then he turned and walked into a house that looked exactly like the McQuinn house, with a patrol car parked in front.

Adam began punching buttons. "Whoa, what a cool game!" he murmured to himself.

On the screen, a group of four Ninja figures crept toward the house. Two of them split off in the direction of the patrol car.

Adam played on, not realizing that the Game Gear had ceased being a toy. Its images were no longer meaningless.

In fact, the scenario on the screen was being played out in real life. Which meant the cops outside were in big danger.

Not to mention Johnny, Adam, and Iggy.

Johnny got up from the couch and pulled Iggy aside. "Don't tell my little bro, but I'm freaked about my dad," he said. "I've got to go nuke a burrito. You want something?"

"Miso curd in black bean oyster sauce." Iggy thought for a moment. "Cancel that. Chips and an Orangina."

Johnny went into the kitchen. He flicked on the light. He turned to the fridge.

And he screamed at the top of his lungs.

There, dressed in black like the specter of death, was Zatch.

Johnny bolted back into the living room. Adam and Iggy were on their feet, their eyes wide with fright. "Johnny, are you okay?" Adam asked.

"Hey, guys," Johnny said angrily, "what's tall,

dark, wears a patch, and always seems to be in my face?"

Zatch's voice rumbled behind him: "You see how easily I could have killed you if I was sent by Colonel Chi?"

All eyes turned. Zatch entered from the kitchen, staring at Johnny.

"Yeah, like that's a *big* challenge," Adam taunted him. "I'm eleven years old. Why don't you just give yourself a big pat on the back?"

"My point is," Zatch continued, "the police cannot help you against him." Suddenly he tensed. "Quiet!"

Johnny, Adam, and Iggy jumped.

"Wow," Adam said, "once again, hats off to the guy who can scare the kids."

"*Shhhh!*" Zatch insisted. He flicked the living room light switch, plunging the room into darkness.

From Adam's Game Gear, a dim light showed two Ninjas attacking the patrol car in front of the house. Around the house itself were about *thirty* Ninjas.

Zatch went to the front window. "Look," he said, gesturing toward the street.

Adam looked up from the Game Gear. He could see two cops slumped over in the front seat of their car.

His heart jumped. He stared at his Game Gear as if it were a lit bomb. *It's some weird kind of crystal ball,* he thought.

Quickly he pulled his thumbs away from the controls, but the figures kept moving.

In a frightened, meek voice, Adam said, "Could we, like, go back to beginners' level?"

Zatch began darting around, shutting all the lights on the ground floor.

Adam gulped. There was no doubt about it. It was sweating time.

Chapter 8

"*QUICKLY!*"

Zatch's whisper had a life-or-death urgency. No one was making fun of him now. Crouching low, he led the boys to the back of the house. Adam held tightly to his Game Gear. He had a feeling he'd need it.

Johnny, Adam, and Iggy went into the bedroom, but Zatch paused in the kitchen for moment. Thinking fast, he grabbed a box of emergency candles from a shelf. He lit one candle and set it on the floor a few feet from the oven. Then he turned on all four burners and blew out the flames.

Gas was spewing into the room. Now there was no time to lose.

Zatch ran into the bedroom—but someone else had gotten there first. The three boys were huddled against the back wall as a Ninja advanced on them.

Whack! Zatch sent a flying kick into the Ninja's head. The Ninja rolled with it and came up ready to fight. But Zatch became a whirl of slashing arms and legs. And when he stopped whirling, the Ninja lay motionless on the floor.

The three boys sat there, stunned at the display. "Come on!" Zatch said.

They leaped to their feet. Zatch helped them out the bedroom window—first Adam, then Johnny, then Iggy.

Adam looked at his Game Gear. The screen showed two Ninjas sneaking around the corner, ready to attack.

"Zatch!" Adam whispered.

Before Adam could say another word, or even point a finger, Zatch spun around to his blind side. He caught both Ninjas with two powerful kicks.

The coast was clear—for now. Time to bolt.

Zatch, Johnny, Adam, and Iggy all ran for their lives. They zigzagged through the dark streets of Venice, along canal banks, through backyards, wherever Zatch led.

As they approached the beach, Adam glanced at his Game Gear again. The onscreen Ninjas had infested the house like ants in a picnic basket.

Finally they slowed down. Now the rhythm of the breaking waves was the only sound louder than the boys' panting.

Adam looked back in the direction of their house. This adventure was getting way too serious. "When do you think we'll be able to go back home?" he asked.

"Your home," Zatch said softly, "is Patu San."

"Our home is that house back there in Ocean Park!" Johnny replied.

"I don't think you want to go back there," Iggy said. "I kept an eye on Long John Silver when he was in the kitchen. He left the gas on. *Real* bright. I mean, what if the house blows up?"

BOOOOOOOOOMMMMMMM!

Iggy froze. His face sank. Johnny and Adam stared in shock.

When Johnny finally spoke, his voice was hoarse with disbelief. "That was our home. You blew up our home."

"I had no choice," Zatch said. "Now you have no choice but to come with me. It is your destiny."

"You had no choice? You're totally insane!" Johnny could hold in his rage no longer. He lunged for Zatch. He wanted to kill him.

Zatch calmly reached out and put an armlock on Johnny.

"Get your raspy hands off my bro!" Adam shouted.

He jumped at Zatch, but Zatch grabbed him, too.

Johnny and Adam struggled against the older man's iron grip. "Be still, Your Highnesses," Zatch urged. "You must understand there is no turning back. Your lives can never be the same again."

The brothers stopped fighting. The truth was dawning on them both. Their father was missing, their house was history, and some goons in black pajamas were after their lives. Zatch was right. Everything was different now.

Zatch was no replacement for Mac, but he was all they had right now.

"But what about our dad?" Adam asked.

"I will help you find Mac," Zatch answered. "That, too, is part of your destiny."

Iggy slowly turned his gaze from the house. His face was still bone-white, his mouth still ajar. A look of horrible guilt was in his eyes. "I can't believe I did that," he whispered.

Zatch gave Iggy a quick glance. "But what of this one, the commoner?" he asked Johnny and Adam.

"Why don't you just blow him up?" Adam suggested.

"Yo, Iggs," Johnny called out, "maybe you better head on home."

"I am responsible for the destruction of my best buds' personal property," Iggy said.

"What are you talking about?" Johnny was annoyed now. This was not the time to be getting weird. "You didn't do anything!"

"Don't you get it?" Iggy said, pacing frantically. "Something has happened. Every time I say 'What if,' it comes true! I can't deal with this responsibility. But what if I lose this power? Then I—" He groaned and slapped his forehead. "Oh, god, what have I done? I just said 'What if I lose my power?' I am the stupidest menace the earth has ever known!"

Zatch watched him, expressionless. "You keep him to amuse you, yes?" he asked. "Like a boy would keep a monkey or a snake?"

"Look," Johnny replied, "we can't just go 'hasta' and leave him. Those quimbies saw him with us. They'll come after him. He's got to come with us."

50 ▬▬

They all watched Iggy, who was still muttering to himself, oblivious to everyone else. Zatch sighed. Duty was duty, and he had to obey the crown princes. If they wanted to save this bizarre and useless creature, so be it.

No one had said it was going to be easy.

From all directions, police cars screeched to a stop in front of the McQuinn house. Actually, the McQuinn *wreckage* was a better description. Only a wooden shell was left of the exterior. Inside were hulking piles of charred and twisted material. Already officers had cordoned off the area with yellow tape. A few had gone inside to sift among the embers.

Lieutenant Spence stood out front, sipping coffee. In his years on the force, he had learned to hide his emotions. Zip them right up and not let anybody in. That was the way to get the job done.

But he was having a hard time hiding them now. They were just kids—even the one pretending to be an uncle. They hadn't had *lives* yet. And now . . .

"Somebody was in that house when it blew up," Spence said to a policeman guarding the house. "But the coroner's going to have to say if it was those kids or not."

He turned to see Sergeant Bork walking toward him. Something small and black was in his right hand.

"What have you got?" Spence asked.

"The plot sickens." Bork held out his hand to reveal a charred throwing star. "If it *was* those kids, they weren't alone. Spence, if I were you, I'd set up a cot in the squad room."

Spence sighed. *Vacation?* Maybe next Christmas. He was in this for the long haul.

Chapter 9

IN THE DUNGEON of Sri Wan, Colonel Chi awaited news of his warriors. But Chi was not one to wait idly. On the contrary, he would have a little *fun*. With delicate but powerful strokes, he sharpened his electric carving knife. Smiling, he handed it to Manchu.

Manchu took it gleefully. He turned to his intended victim, a helpless prisoner. Chi stepped aside for a choice view.

With a sudden lurch, Chi fell to the floor, inches from the dungeon's moat. Below, two crocodiles eyed him hungrily.

Chi looked down at his foot. It was tangled in the electric knife's extension cord.

Manchu walked over with a guilty smile. "Sorry," he grunted, unwrapping the cord.

As Chi stood up, he pointed to the battery pack on his chest. "Manchu," he growled, "it almost got wet."

Manchu quickly checked the indicator on the pack. "Your batteries are dry, Colonel," he said.

"Maybe you need to be reminded of how important it is that they stay that way!" Chi thundered.

He grabbed the knife and turned it on. Manchu cowered. Slowly, with a sinister grin, Chi lowered the knife toward his assistant.

Bleeeeeeeep!

At the sound of the phone, Chi stopped. Manchu's terrified look disappeared. He sighed with relief, wiping droplets of cold sweat from his forehead.

Chi took the electric knife with him to the phone. He passed a prisoner, sprawled out on a table under a suspended bed of downward-pointing spikes. The bed was held up by a rope—and the prisoner tensed with fright at the sight of Chi's knife.

Chi ignored him. He yanked the receiver off the hook. "Hello!"

His eyes narrowed as a nervous voice from California answered him. "Zatch is there?" Chi roared, his teeth clenched with fury. "I should have known. *Kill them!*"

Beep.

"Hold on a second," Chi continued. "That's my Call Waiting." He clicked the receiver hook. "Yes? . . . Kill them. Kill them immediately."

He clicked again and got back to his original call. "Now, where were we? Oh, yes . . . *kill them!* Send more men to Los Angeles—by coach. Send the Tiger Ninjas, my most efficient killers. The boys are alive. I can feel it. *I want them dead!*" He glanced toward Manchu, who gave a tiny wave. "Oh, yes . . . and Manchu says hi."

Manchu. Chi had some unfinished business

with him. He slammed the receiver down and clutched the knife in his tiger claw.

Manchu stepped back in fear. Chi adjusted the knobs on his battery pack.

Dzzzzit. His arm went wild. It pulled Chi around the room. He fumbled at the controls, cursing. The knife sliced through the air in all directions. With a clean *shhhiink,* it cut the rope that suspended the bed of spikes.

The claw stopped twitching. The spikes fell. The prisoner shrieked.

Chi looked at the bloody mess, then at Manchu. With a triumphant nod, he said, "And let that be a lesson to you!"

Johnny had never been more grossed out in his life. They were in the middle of L.A., but it might as well have been some poverty-stricken, disease-riddled country.

A rat skittered into the dim light of the alleyway. It twitched its nose twice, then disappeared behind a mound of rotting garbage.

Stealthily Zatch led the three boys through the alley, to the back door of a restaurant. Above it were the words PATU SANI IMPERIAL PALACE RESTAURANT.

"We will be safe here," Zatch said. "You will find that your subjects love you and are loyal to you."

"Stylin'," Adam replied. "We're the princes of take-out."

He and Johnny followed Zatch inside. In the kitchen stood a skinny man with bad teeth and an ill-fitting suit. Zatch whispered something to him in the Patu Sani language.

The man's face brightened. He turned to the boys with a smile and chattered something totally unrecognizable.

"They do not speak Patu Sani, Gum-Bey," Zatch explained to the man. Then, turning to Johnny and Adam, Zatch said, "He was prostrating himself to you, to show his loyalty. His name is Gum-Bey."

"As in Po-Key's friend?" Johnny said with a smile. "That's my bro, Adam. And that's Iggy."

"That's *King* Iggy," Iggy added. "How's it hanging, Gumby?"

Looking a little confused—but still smiling—Gum-Bey bowed low. Then he gestured for them all to follow.

As they walked through the kitchen, Zatch said, "There will be trouble, Gum-Bey. You should know that before you take us in."

Johnny didn't like the sound of that. And from the ashen looks on Adam's and Iggy's faces, they weren't crazy about it, either.

"Trouble?" Gum-Bey said. "Trouble does not worry me. His Highness Yow-ni is to be my daughter's husband. This is a day of rejoicing. I must tell the others."

Huh?

"Whoa, gel, Gumby!" Johnny said. "What do you mean?"

Too late. Grinning ecstatically, Gum-Bey stepped through the door that led into the restaurant.

Johnny turned to Zatch. "What did he mean, I was going to be, like, his daughter's husband?"

"It means you're not going to be calling him Gumby anymore," Adam said. "You're going to call him Dad."

"Technically," Iggy chimed in, "he'll be your Gumby-in-law."

"The wedding was agreed to by your father and Gum-Bey," Zatch said, "when you were children."

"Great. I get to marry the offspring of *that*"—he pointed in Gum-Bey's direction—"and the woman who would marry that?"

"You judge him by his physical appearance," Zatch said, "but Gum-Bey's heart is good."

"Well, that's probably because he eats a lot of fish and rice and watches his red meat intake," Johnny replied, "but that is still no reason to marry his daughter. I mean, when I get knotted, it is going to be to an A-One Steak Sauce Betty."

"Who is this Betty?" Zatch asked.

"It's an expression," Adam said, "meaning, like, All-American Girl."

Zatch shook his head at Johnny. "You are superficial, and your values are only skin deep."

"Yeah, but that doesn't mean I don't have good taste," Johnny said.

"You will learn humility, Your Highness."

With those words, Zatch turned and walked into the restaurant. The room was large but dingy. In one corner, three ancient Patu Sani musicians sat with strange stringed instruments. They looked as though they hadn't moved in years. Old, yellowing posters hung on the walls, and gray pathways were worn into the linoleum-tile floors by years of scurrying waiters.

And were they ever scurrying now! A team of them moved tables around, squeezing in extra ones wherever they could. Gum-Bey was by the kitchen, yelling into a phone while shouting instructions at his workers.

Zatch, Johnny, Adam, and Iggy were led to a long table against one of the walls. There, waiters were laying out expensive-looking place settings.

Within minutes, the place was swarming with customers. All of them stared at Johnny and Adam, whispering among themselves. Johnny felt embarrassed. He knew he should have paid more attention to geography. Here were all these refugees from Patu San—his subjects, supposedly—and he had never even heard of the place!

As the dumplings were served, Johnny forgot about his embarrassment. His mouth was watering. One major problem, though. Chopsticks. He hated them. He looked over to see Adam and Iggy playing with theirs, kicking them up together as if they were dancers' legs in a chorus line.

Gum-Bey walked up to a small podium by the head table. Instantly the restaurant quieted down.

"Long have we dreamed of this day," Gum-Bey announced, "when we could welcome our all-wise, all-knowing monarchs once again, as the prophecies foretold. They have returned, and our future is secure."

Johnny had joined the chopsticks kick line. He

Three dudes, Johnny, Adam, and Iggy,
begin their day California style.

Squank! It's an invasion.

Don't fear, dudes. Zatch is here to keep his eyes, uh—his eye on things.

After an epic transformation from surf rat to Ninja warrior . . .

... the four dudes set off in search of their nemesis.

Found him . . .

And guess what?
He has their dad!

The long journey to rescue Mac seems interminable.

What if Iggy
could fast-forward
to all the action?

Then Johnny would be a hero.

And he'd get all the babes.

And he'd set his people free.

THE END.

glanced up to see Gum-Bey staring at them, looking bewildered.

Quickly Johnny, Adam, and Iggy dropped the sticks and bowed to the people.

"Please, Your Highness Yow-ni," Gum-Bey said, "the people hunger for your words."

"I'd be amped to say a few words." It was a lie. Johnny had no idea what to say. He got up and walked to the podium. A waiter passed by with a tray full of fortune cookies.

Idea.

Johnny grabbed a handful of cookies and brought them to the podium. As he smiled at the crowd, he caught a glimpse of the three ancient musicians. "Hey, let's give it up for the band!" he shouted.

Adam and Iggy pretended to pull out lighters and hold them in the air. The musicians looked baffled. The crowd stayed absolutely silent.

I'm dying up here, Johnny thought. "Okay . . . some words of wisdom from your new leader."

He hid the fortune cookies below the podium. One by one, he quietly cracked them open and read the fortunes: " 'You will travel to exotic places where you will make many friends . . . ' "

Crrrack.

"And 'your careful planning will lead to prosperous business ventures . . . ' "

Crrrack.

" 'Do not let your need for material security keep you from taking a chance on your dreams.' And always remember . . . "

Crrrack.

" 'You will meet a tall, handsome man and he will break your heart.' Thank you."

The crowd stared blankly. One person began to applaud. Then, shakily, the rest of them joined in.

Gum-Bey stepped up to the podium. "Yes. And now, Your Highness, for you and all of us a most joyful moment as you meet your future bride, Ro-May."

The musicians began playing. All eyes looked toward a beaded archway to Johnny's left. Through the archway came a young woman, her face covered by a dark veil that hung from an ornate headdress.

Adam leaned over to his brother. "You know what they say," he whispered. "If the chick's got a veil, dude better bail!"

"Yeah," Johnny said, "if they cover her face, pick up the pace!"

Ro-May walked slowly through a sea of smiling, expectant faces. Johnny could see tears in the eyes of some of the Patu Sanis as she stopped in front of his table.

Beaming with pride, Gum-Bey pulled off his daughter's veil. Johnny prepared to lose his dumplings at the sight.

Instead he felt a lump catch in his throat. She was gorgeous.

Gorgeous? She was stunning, bodacious, incredible. Her hair was a cascade of black silk, her eyes deep and warm. Her skin took the dingy light of the restaurant and reflected back a hot, luscious amber.

When she smiled at him, Johnny thought his

knees would give in. "Whoa," he said under his breath. "She's not just a Betty. She's an *Elizabeth*."

Gum-Bey took his daughter's hand and placed it in Johnny's.

"Honey," Adam piped up, "I'm going to have to write you a ticket. *Toooo* sexy!"

"Back off, grom, this one's mine," Johnny snapped. When he turned back to Ro-May, he froze. He didn't want to sound overconfident, like Adam. He didn't want to sound dorky, like Iggy.

But what do you say to the most beautiful stranger you have ever seen—who's about to become your wife?

"Uh . . . uh . . . you want to go to the mall sometime?"

Adam groaned. "Way to close the deal, Casanova."

Johnny felt like sinking into the ground. *The mall?* How stupid, how ridiculous, how—

"You do not need to go out," Gum-Bey said in a laughing voice. "Soon you will be married!"

That was when Ro-May spoke for the first time: "And I will be yours forever, Your Highness."

Johnny couldn't help smiling. He felt he'd died and gone to heaven. Adam just stared, slack-jawed.

A little weak in the knees himself, Iggy turned to Zatch. "You think we ought to tell her that Johnny's just the decoy and *I'm* the one she's really going to marry?"

Zatch shot him a murderous look. Fortunately for everyone, Iggy quickly shut up.

Chapter 10

Bleeeeeeeep!

When the phone rang, Colonel Chi was resting from a busy day of torture. His eyes were glued to the TV.

He flicked on the speakerphone. "What word do you have?"

Clear across the world, on a freeway in Los Angeles, a Ninja held a car phone up to his mouth. His face was twisted with frustration and fear. His hands trembled.

Major Snee had never known so much failure. He and Captain Ming had served Colonel Chi flawlessly since the uprising. But since they had been sent to California as assassins, everything had gone wrong. They had been the ones driving the garbage truck, they had been the leaders of the attack on the McQuinn house. Luckily, they'd survived.

But it would not be so easy to survive the wrath of Colonel Chi.

Snee sighed. He wished Captain Ming had been in the driver's seat instead. But he'd left Ming behind at a strategy session. He was alone in the car. He and the voice of Colonel Chi.

"It is as if they had vanished," Snee repeated.

"They did not *vanish*!" Chi bellowed. "They are *boys*—stupid American boys! I can see that you and your men are no match for one lone Imperial Guard. That is why I have sent my Tiger Ninja. No more excuses!"

"There will be no more excuses, my colonel," Snee promised.

"I know," Chi said.

Snee was shaking all over now. There was something in the way Chi had said that. Something almost too calm, too friendly. As if he were holding back a deadly secret.

Snee slammed on the brakes for a red light. His car skidded to a stop.

He didn't notice Captain Ming rising from behind his seat. He barely felt the hard wooden club make contact with his head.

And he didn't even have enough time to say "Good-bye" to Chi before he slumped to the floor in a motionless heap.

With a triumphant grin, Captain Ming jumped into the driver's seat. He grabbed the car phone and said, "Everything is under control."

In the dungeon, Colonel Chi waited for confirmation. When he heard Ming's voice, he smiled. Ming would not let him down.

"Perhaps Zatch and the boys are not alone," Chi said. "Perhaps they have sought allies who mistakenly believe they live far enough away from Patu San to have nothing to fear from me. It is time for the Tiger to prowl once again! That is all."

Chi hung up and turned back to the television—but his tiger claw was stuck to the phone. He yanked hard, to no avail. Grunting with rage, he pulled a second time, a third . . .

Instantly Manchu rushed over with a tool kit. It was going to be another long afternoon.

Johnny McQuinn was jittery. What was happening to his life? Yesterday he was just hanging with the guys, having a great time. Now he had a whole country to worry about. Not to mention a wife-to-be.

Johnny paced the rooftop of the Imperial Palace Restaurant. In the distance, the skyline of downtown L.A. rose like a distant smoggy mountain range. As ugly as it was, he didn't want to leave. Destiny or no destiny, he belonged here. Not on some far-off island where they hadn't discovered snack food or fluoride.

If it weren't for the fact that his dad was missing, Johnny would have said *"hasta"* to Zatch long ago. Well, that wasn't totally true. There was Ro-May to think about.

Ro-May hung over all his thoughts like some miraculous angel. A few hours ago he'd been afraid she'd be a bowser. He'd thought he'd have to use every trick in the book to get out of the marriage.

Now he wanted her. If she'd gone to Surf View

High, he would have spent the year chasing her down. And he would have been joined by every male in the entire school, teachers included.

She was perfect. And she was his. Tom Cruise could fall all over her, and she'd turn away. She *had* to marry Johnny, like it or not.

And that was the problem. Girls who looked like Ro-May never hung out with guys like Johnny. They didn't have to. They reserved all the hunks, and L.A. was the Hunk Capital of America. What if Ro-May couldn't stand him? What if she felt about him the same way he'd felt about her before she lifted the veil? What if she thought *he* was a bowser? Would he be able to look her in the eye every day for the rest of his life, knowing she hated him? It would be one thing if he knew how to be a warrior king, but that was totally ridiculous. All he knew how to do was surf.

He sighed. Ro-May was the type who said what she was supposed to say. Would he ever find out her real feelings?

His eyes caught something moving on the ground. A shadow. Johnny screamed and whirled around.

"Oh! I'm sorry! Did I scare you?"

It was Ro-May. Johnny pulled himself together. He tried to look cool. "Nay. Not even."

Ro-May smiled. "Once you have the weapons of Kwantzu you will have nothing to fear again."

"Are those the 'Amazing Kwantzu Weapons'? The ones that come with the free SaladShooter?"

Ro-May ignored the joke. "The prophecies foretell that it is the chosen one's destiny to find the ancient weapons of Kwantzu. Then you will be invincible, just as surely as I will be yours."

"This is fully weird," Johnny said, shaking his head. "I haven't even started dating yet, and already I'm engaged. You think we could at least hang out first?"

"There is no hanging out necessary, Your Highness. I am yours."

"But you don't even know me."

"I have heard the prophecies. I know you."

"Okay," Johnny said. "What's my favorite color?"

"Blue," Ro-May replied.

"Okay, that was easy." This was absurd. Johnny knew he had to come clean with her, no matter how much it embarrassed him. "Ro-May, I think you should *like* me first."

Ro-May gave him a quizzical look. "It doesn't matter if I like you. It has been decided."

"Nothing's decided. This is America in the nineties. People can all do what they want."

"So what do you want, Your Highness?" Ro-May asked with a shrug.

Johnny exhaled sadly. "I want my home back. I want my life back."

"It may be too late for that," Ro-May replied.

Johnny didn't know what to say. He hung his head and tried to keep his thoughts from becoming a jumble.

Ro-May watched him for a moment, then quietly turned and walked away.

Johnny looked up and followed her with his eyes. "And," he said softly, "I want you to like me."

If she heard him, he never knew.

Chapter 11

THE VICTIM WAS TALKING. In rapid Patu Sani. The paramedics swarmed around him with bandages and antiseptic.

He had been attacked in an alley not far from the Imperial Palace Restaurant. And he looked scared out of his wits.

Lieutenant Spence listened impatiently as a Patu Sani cop translated the victim's story:

" ' . . . And it was into the arms of Mac, a former American sailor, that the two children were entrusted.' "

"Yeah, yeah, yeah," Spence said. "But does he know where the kids are now?"

"He's too afraid to talk," the cop said.

Spence threw up his hands. "A twenty-five-minute story and *now* he's afraid to talk!"

He walked away, disgusted. All he needed was to lose those kids, now that he knew they were still alive. If *that* happened, he might have a much longer vacation than he'd wanted.

Without pay.

But Johnny, Adam, and Iggy weren't far away. They had decided to sneak out for a walk.

As they shuffled dejectedly through the Patu Sani section of L.A., Adam stared at his Game Gear. "Hey, Johnny," he said, "look at this!"

The screen showed Ninjas breaking into the Imperial Palace Restaurant. As Adam worked the controls, the scene shifted inside. Now the Ninjas were ambushing Johnny, Adam, Iggy, and Ro-May.

Adam pressed the attack button. His onscreen self reached into a fish tank and shoved a live octopus into a Ninja's face.

500 BONUS POINTS! the screen flashed.

"Whoa!" Adam cried out.

But Johnny's eyes were focused on the entrance of the restaurant, a half-block away. The door crashed open, and waiters began running out.

"Help! Somebody help me, please!" Ro-May's voice screamed from inside.

Johnny sprinted into the restaurant. Ro-May struggled against a sea of black—at least six Tiger Ninjas, including Captain Ming.

"Hey!" Johnny shouted. "Get your hands off my Betty-to-be!"

Adam and Iggy ran up behind him. Captain Ming glared at them. "It's them!" he cried out.

The Tiger Ninjas released Ro-May and turned toward Johnny.

"Uh, Ro-May," Johnny said with a nervous gulp,

"you know what would be great? If you ran like crazy and got Winkie, the one-eyed black belt."

Adam held up his Game Gear and whispered to Johnny, "We've got nothing to worry about, bro. It's our destiny. Besides, I've played this level before."

The Tiger Ninjas advanced. Ro-May bolted through the back door. Iggy dived under the nearest table. Adam headed for the fish tank.

Johnny backed up. His leg hit the corner of a dim sum cart. Quickly he grabbed the cart and shoved it into the Ninjas' path.

They jumped away, but not in time. Three of them sprawled to the floor. A fourth tried to leap over the cart—and fell face first into the dim sum.

Johnny let go. The cart rolled to the other end of the room, smashing the Ninja against the wall.

In a far corner of the room, another Ninja loomed over Adam, poised for attack. Adam reached into the fish tank, closed his fingers around a live octopus, and hurled it.

It landed with a *splat* in the Ninja's face. "Five hundred bonus points!" Adam screamed.

Under a nearby table, Iggy began mumbling to himself. "Power, come back to me. *What if* I could actually control the outcome of this fight?"

Crrrrassh!

Crrrrassh!

Johnny hurled one china plate after another. He was desperate. The Ninjas ducked away easily, with lightning reflexes. They fanned out left and right.

Soon Johnny was trapped. A black wall of Ninjas

surrounded him. Shoulder to shoulder, they advanced, their faces twisted with anger and revenge.

Angriest of all was Captain Ming himself. He stepped forward with a cocky grin. Then, without warning, he lunged. His arm sliced the air with a lethal swiftness.

Johnny stiffened with the icy fear of death. His mind went blank.

Thunk.

Johnny's arm snapped upward, as if it had a mind of its own. It blocked Ming's thrust perfectly.

Ming was stunned. Johnny gaped at his arm in shock.

Quickly Ming struck again. Johnny blocked with his left arm, then shot out a karate chop with his right.

Thwap!

The blow struck Ming at the base of the neck. His mouth opened to a perfect O, and he spiraled to the floor.

Johnny held up his hand in awe. "Whoa . . . how did you do that?"

But there was no time to question. Around him, the other Ninjas closed in. Johnny hopped on a table. His feet landed squarely in the middle of a Lazy Susan.

He pushed off with one leg, and the Lazy Susan began to spin.

Whack! Whack! Whack! Whack! Whack! Whack!

With the speed of an automatic weapon, Johnny's leg connected with the jaw of each Ninja.

One by one they fell like swatted flies.

"Thank you!" Iggy was shouting under the table. "The master returns!"

But Johnny was not out of the woods. Ming was stirring to consciousness. He rose to his feet, his eyes burning with murderous hate. He reached behind him. Out of a small black backpack he yanked a weapon.

Johnny's eyes bulged. It was the most fearsome thing he'd ever seen—a tiger's paw, with enormous claws that glinted in the light.

Johnny held a chair in front of him. Ming slashed once, twice, three times.

The chair clattered to the floor in splinters.

Johnny gulped. "I am in deep caca," he murmured.

Ming laughed. He raised his arm, flexing his claws. Johnny knew there would be no blocking this—unless he wanted his arm cut off at the elbow. He backed away.

His back thumped against a wall. There was no place to go now. Ming slashed like a wild animal.

Johnny did the only thing he could. He closed his eyes and prepared to be killed.

Chapter 12

HE DIDN'T FEEL THE CLAW. In fact, he felt nothing. Was this what death was like? So painless, so—

"Yeeeeaaaaaahhhhhh—"

It was Ming's voice. It sounded choked and furious. Johnny's eyes sprang open.

There was a reason he felt nothing. Ming's arm was frozen in mid-swing. A fist was wrapped around it.

The fist belonged to Zatch.

Zatch swung Ming around. He lashed a kick to Ming's abdomen, a fist to his face.

Ming fought back, but it was too late. With two swift kicks, Zatch sent him hurtling into the air.

He landed with a loud splash in the restaurant's lobster tank.

The Imperial Palace was silent now, save for some snapping noises in the tank. Johnny smiled at Zatch.

"Whoa!" Adam shouted, holding up his Game Gear. "I beat my best score!"

Iggy crawled out from under the table. "Seriously, don't thank me. It's the least I could do as your monarch."

"It was incredible!" Johnny said to Zatch. "For a minute there, I almost had these guys. Did you know I could do this?"

He chopped with his arm, kicked with his leg. The moves were there, and they looked awesome.

"Your destiny is drawing near," Zatch said. "Soon you will be a great warrior."

"If he's a great warrior," Adam said, "what about me?"

"You will be a seer of visions," Zatch replied. "Close your eyes and tell me what you see."

Adam jammed his eyes shut. "I see you leading thousands victoriously into battle and becoming a national hero."

Zatch looked amazed. "Really?"

"Oh, my god!" Adam cried. "You're wearing a dress!"

"What's this?" Zatch said.

Adam smiled. "Rank!"

"Johnny!" Ro-May called, running in through the back door. "Are you all right?"

Johnny beamed. "You mean, you really care?"

"You are the symbol of the revolution," Ro-May replied.

"You're really an incurable romantic, you know that?" Johnny said with a sigh.

Gum-Bey followed his daughter inside. His face was grim. "We have received word from the Resistance. Yow-ni, they have taken your father to the Dungeon of Sri Wan."

"Sri Wan!" Ro-May exclaimed. "That is the Fortress of Death!"

Silence hung over the room like smog. All eyes were on Johnny. He knew what Gum-Bey wanted. It was the same thing every Patu Sani exile wanted. The return of the princes, the overthrow of the dictator. Ridiculous. Totally wacko.

Until now. Now Mac was in danger. It was time to take a stand.

Johnny turned to his brother, his eyes set with determination. "Let's go get our dad."

He ran to the restaurant's front door, but stopped short. Through the window he saw Lieutenant Spence's car pulling up with a couple of black-and-whites.

"Squank," Johnny said. "It's Spence. We have to get out of here."

"But he wanted to help us," Adam said.

"Adam, we have to help ourselves. Besides, he's not going to fall for the Uncle Iggy bit again."

"How about Aunt Iggy?" Iggy piped up.

"Come!" Ro-May said. "We will go out the back way."

"Take my van," Gum-Bey insisted.

They ran to the back alley, where a dilapidated van was parked. Gum-Bey kissed his daughter, then embraced the others.

Quickly Ro-May, Johnny, Adam, and Iggy all piled in. Zatch climbed into the driver's seat and drove away.

In front of the restaurant, Lieutenant Spence watched the van turn onto the main street. He smiled wearily. "Okay, kids, enough's enough," he muttered. "Papa's exhausted. I'm going to take you in to the nice warm station house. Then I'm going beddy-bye."

Quietly he pulled into the traffic and began following the van.

By the time Zatch parked in San Pedro Harbor, the sun had set. A rusting old freighter sat on the water like a tired monster. Deckhands loaded crates up its creaky gangplank.

"Follow me," Zatch said.

The van emptied. Zatch led Ro-May, Johnny, Adam, and Iggy up the gangplank and onto the ship.

"What about the deckhands?" Adam asked.

Zatch turned and gave him a wink. "They're on our side."

In the parking lot, Lieutenant Spence rolled to a stop. His headlights were off, and he'd parked in the shadow of a concrete stairway.

He'd seen where Zatch and the kids had gone—and he knew he didn't have much time. He hopped out and ran for the gangplank.

It began to rise the moment Spence stepped onto it. He held on for dear life, and managed to climb aboard.

Spence planted his feet on deck. He was safe—and well positioned. The McQuinn brothers were a few yards away, leaning over the railing next to two other kids. They hadn't seen him. "Johnny! Adam!" he called out.

The four of them whirled around. Spence moved closer, eyeing the one who looked like the boys' "uncle" he had seen at the house. "Hey," Spence said, "aren't you—"

"Hey, you kids, turn down that hi-fi or no icebox tonight!" Iggy suddenly shouted at Johnny and Adam. Then he turned to Spence with a smile. "Hi. Uncle Iggy. I'm thirty-seven. Nice to meet you."

"Lieutenant Spence," Johnny said, "what are you doing here?"

"Saving you from being kidnapped, Jack," Spence replied. "Let's get out of here, quick."

"Squank. We're not being kidnapped," Adam said. "We're going to start the revolution. Everything's cool."

Spence glared at him. "*Everything's cool?* I've been hauling myself all over town, stepping on Ninjas of every shape and size—so everything is most definitely *not* cool!"

"Lieutenant . . . "

The voice behind him was low and unfamiliar. Spence felt a hand on his shoulder. He turned around to see a patch-eyed man inches away from him.

Before he could react, the man said, "Good night," and squeezed.

Spence felt his knees buckle and his eyes close. He tried to fight the feeling for a moment, but stopped. Sleep was pulling him down. Sweet, gentle sleep. To tell the truth, it didn't feel too bad.

" 'Night," Spence said as he crumpled to the deck with a thud.

Chapter 13

"ALL RIGHT, MAC, your approximate weight?" Colonel Chi punched in some numbers on his computer. "One hundred seventy pounds, one hundred seventy-five?"

Mac struggled against his wrist and leg restraints. He was helpless. In moments the rack would begin to pull him apart. He looked up into the grinning, hideous face of Manchu, who was leaning over him.

"I'll never tell you anything, Chi!" Mac snapped. "You ugly, metal-headed—"

Whack! Manchu cuffed him on the side of the head.

"And what is your height?" Chi asked. "It doesn't have to be exact. It's going to change."

"Do what you want, Chi," Mac said. "You'll never find out where my boys are."

"Really?" Chi smiled confidently. "I've got a surprise, Macko. My sources tell me your boys are on their way here to join their daddy."

"Rrrraaaagghh—" Mac lurched desperately against his straps, but Manchu slugged him again.

As Mac sank back, Chi laughed. He turned to a mirror to admire himself.

Instantly his smile turned to a scowl. He pulled back his tiger paw and struck hard.

The mirror tinkled to the floor in jagged pieces. "Oops," Chi said. "Bad luck."

For days, the freighter slowly plowed the ocean. For days, Johnny played shuffleboard, Hacky Sack, and Ultimate with his brother, his friend, his fiancée, and his mentor.

Several times a day, Zatch went below deck to check on Lieutenant Spence. He had used Spence's own handcuffs to shackle him to a metal pole.

On the last scheduled day of the trip, all of them stood expectantly by the railing. "We should be able to see the coast of Patu San," Ro-May said, squinting into the distance.

"Pardon me, but I haven't seen daylight, let alone land, for days."

Everyone turned at the sound of Spence's voice.

Spence smiled at them, holding up his open handcuffs.

"How did you get out?" Johnny asked.

"I had a key," Spence replied.

"Where?" Johnny said. "We searched you."

Spence shrugged. "I swallowed it last Tuesday."

"That's incredible," Johnny said. "How did you know you were going to need it?"

"I swallow it every Tuesday."

Johnny figured it was time to stop asking questions. He didn't want to hear the details. "You're not going to stop us, Lieutenant."

"I'm not going to try," Spence answered. "I'm going to join you."

"You are?" Iggy asked.

Adam looked flabbergasted. "Why?"

"Look," Spence said, "I just lost my girl, I haven't had a vacation in seventeen months, and I am in heavy need of some laughs."

They all smiled at that, even Zatch.

"Besides," Spence went on, "I just have a feeling that going with you guys . . . "

He paused, and Zatch quietly finished his sentence. " . . . is your destiny."

Spence nodded.

"Look!" Ro-May pointed to a dark smudge of land in the distance. "Patu San!"

As the freighter came nearer, they all ran below deck to the supply room. There, along with food and emergency supplies, were boxes of Patu Sani clothing.

Spence picked out a traditional villager's outfit. Zatch, Johnny, Adam, and Iggy found uniforms of the Imperial Guard. The uniforms were embroidered with the symbol of the fire-breathing dragon.

Solemnly they changed, casting aside their old clothing forever. The revolution was about to begin.

The sun was rising as they rowed in to the Patu Sani coast in a rubber lifeboat. They had landed on the uninhabited side of the island. Quietly they all stepped onto the shore. Zatch lifted out a backpack full of supplies, then pushed the boat back out to sea.

"What about the boat?" Spence asked. "Won't it be spotted?"

"I have drilled a hole in it," Zatch replied. "Soon it will sink to the bottom of the ocean."

"Seriously," Iggy said, "that's an excellent place to hide it."

"Yeah, but what if we're getting hammered and we have to bail?" Johnny asked.

Zatch looked him grimly in the eye. "We shall be victorious or in our graves."

"There's no gray area with you, is there?" Adam said. "The glass is either half full or we're dead."

Zatch ignored Adam. He turned and began walking up a steep hill. Ro-May, Johnny, Adam, and Iggy scampered behind him.

At the top they all stopped. The hill had flattened into a ridge. Below them, shrouded in a thin morning mist, was a dense green jungle. Beyond it lay a small village. Wisps of smoke curled to sky above it.

"That is the village of Mee Grob," Ro-May said.

"While in Patu San," Johnny intoned in the voice of a game show announcer, "guests of the revolution stay at the Mee Grob Hilton!"

"The Mee Grob Hilton," Iggy added, "serving strange things in shells since 1207!"

Zatch shook his head in disapproval. "It is the birthplace of a great holy man."

"Then I've got to get a T-shirt," Adam said.

"I can see the morning cooking fires," Zatch said. "There will be many supporters there who will join us. And then we shall go up to the caves of Kwantzu, the caves of the ancients."

"What's there?" Adam asked.

Zatch looked gravely from Johnny to Adam. "Your inheritance."

"Money?" Spence said.

"No, something not even money can buy," Zatch answered. "The knives of Kwantzu."

Iggy rolled his eyes. "Oh, yeah, seriously. That's something money can't buy—knives. I once went to a cutlery store and said, 'Here's a hundred thousand dollars. Can I buy a knife?' And they said, 'No, money cannot buy knives.' Gee, I guess that's why I hardly ever see them around."

Iggy blabbered on, but Zatch ignored him. Cautiously stepping over the ridge, Zatch beckoned to the others.

They began climbing downward and into the jungle.

For hours they trekked through the undergrowth, in sweltering heat. The only sounds were the snapping of branches, heavy breathing, and Iggy's voice.

" . . . And on the third day of the expedition," he was saying to no one in particular, "they came across a giant rubber plant. Unfortunately, they could not cut it down, for as we know, money can't buy knives. Walking around the plant, they continued on to the shores of . . . "

Zatch turned to Lieutenant Spence. "Is there no way you can shut this chattering monkey up?"

"I'd cut him," Spence replied, "but I don't have a knife."

They walked on, trying to concentrate. Before long, the smell of the smoke from Mee Grob became overpowering. *Morning cooking fires?* Johnny thought. *What are they cooking, a whole herd of yaks?*

As they approached the village, even Iggy fell silent. All of Mee Grob was smoking—all that was left of it, that is.

Johnny felt sick to his stomach. The entire village was in ashes. Charred remains of houses lay in twisted black piles. Frightened animals wandered among the rubble, their fur singed. Dazed and horror-stricken, a few survivors picked through the wreckage.

An old blind man wandered aimlessly, talking softly to himself. Zatch walked over to him and took his arm.

Ro-May shook her head. Her face was etched with anguish. "Who would do something like this?" she said.

"I'll give you three guesses," Spence replied.

They watched Zatch talk to the blind man. As he returned, Ro-May called out, "Why did they spare the old man and those others?"

"So there would be someone left alive to tell," Zatch replied.

"Tell what?" Johnny asked. "Tell who?"

Spence had an answer. "Tell anyone who would help us that this is what will happen to them."

Zatch nodded in agreement. "There is only one thing to do—go on to the caves of Kwantzu."

They left the village and went back into the jungle. In the distance, a mountain rose above the timberline. As the sun moved higher in the sky, Zatch led the others up the steep slope.

In the midday heat, mammoth mosquitoes began to attack them. They trudged through thorny undergrowth, slapping away flies and dodging the snakes that hung from the trees. They crossed rickety bridges, forded swift-running streams.

To Iggy, the flies were the worst. His arms were constantly swatting, and he complained the whole way.

Finally, Zatch walked over to him. In seven quick barehanded motions, he grabbed every mosquito that hovered around Iggy's head. Then he held out their squashed bodies to Iggy. "Enjoy," he said with a sly smile.

Iggy shut up the rest of the way.

At the top of the mountain they all stopped. The jungle had cleared, and the entire island stretched out gloriously below them. At the very highest point stood an enormous rock. An altar had been carved out of its side, and on the altar was a statue.

A statue of a two-headed, fire-breathing dragon. The same dragon that was on Adam's Game Gear. The same dragon that was embroidered on Johnny's and Zatch's uniforms.

Monkeys skittered around the statue, jabbering angrily.

"Kwantzu," Zatch announced. "The entrance to the cave itself, however, is hidden."

"So how do we find it?" Johnny asked.

"It is not my destiny to find it," Zatch replied.

"Of course not," Iggy said. "I am the king. Okay, *what if* I found the entrance?"

They all spread out. Adam flipped on his Game Gear. Only one word appeared on the screen:

COLD

He began walking. The words changed:

COLDER . . . MUCH COLDER . . . FREEZING

Before Adam could turn back, a monkey grabbed the Game Gear from his hand. "Whoa!" Adam cried.

The monkey ran to the dragon statue and began jumping up and down. Adam ran up to him, grabbed back the Game Gear, and glanced at the screen:

MUCH WARMER . . . HOT!

"You know, don't you?" Adam shouted. "Where is it, boy?"

The monkey pointed to the dragon's tail. Adam touched it, then gave it a strong yank.

Johnny ran up beside him. Suddenly he felt himself shaking, as if there had been an earthquake. He looked at Adam, who looked at the monkey.

Then the earth below Johnny opened up.

He tried to leap upward, but it was too late. Shrieking with terror, Johnny plunged into a hole of unending blackness.

Chapter 14

*T*HUD.

"Yeeeeooow!"

Adam, Ro-May, Spence, Zatch, and the monkey all ran to the edge of the hole. "Johnny, are you okay?" Ro-May called down.

"Yeah," Johnny's voice wafted up. "But I landed on this mondo mound of jewels and treasure."

"Really?" Zatch said.

"Rank!" Johnny called back.

Everyone sighed, relieved that Johnny was alive.

Finally Iggy came to the hole, a look of triumph on his face. "Opened it!" he yelled to Johnny. "I get half!"

The monkey knew better. He turned to Adam and raised his hand.

Adam smiled and gave him a high five.

"We will join you," Zatch said to Johnny. He pulled two torches out of his pack and gave one to Spence.

In the torchlight, Zatch could see a long ramp that spiraled downward. The two men led the others onto it. They all slid down, joining Johnny at the bottom of the hole.

Johnny's eyes were beginning to adjust. This was no ordinary hole. It was a huge cave that seemed to stretch underground for miles.

Eeeeek-eek-eek-eek!

Johnny flinched at the squeaking noise above.

"Hey, birds," Adam said, looking up at the shadows darting right and left.

"No," Zatch replied. "Bats."

Johnny's stomach did a flipflop. He followed close behind Zatch, until an amber glow appeared in the distance.

The glow got brighter and fuller as they approached. It was a Buddha, made of solid gold. Beyond it, the path turned sharply right.

The turn led them into a small alcove. Ro-May let out a gasp. Two jeweled crowns shone magnificently in the torchlight. They were perched on a stone shelf, about ankle-high. Hanging on the wall above them was a dazzling display of weapons. Nunchucks, throwing stars, fighting poles, and a sword—all were studded with jewels.

But what caught Johnny's eye was a massive golden double-headed trident. It was the most fearsome object he had ever seen.

"The weapons of Kwantzu, just as the prophecies foretold," Zatch said in a respectful whisper. "What Excalibur was to King Arthur in the legends of the West, these weapons will be to Your Highness."

Johnny swallowed. These things looked as if

they belonged in a museum. The only thing missing was a PLEASE DO NOT TOUCH sign.

Zatch pulled the sword and the trident from the wall. He held them out to Johnny.

Johnny wanted to back away. The weapons seemed to pulse with some kind of weird inner energy. They scared him, but at the same time they pulled him forward like magnets.

Zatch placed Johnny's hands firmly around the sword and the trident. Then he clasped his own hands around Johnny's.

"Four thousand years of blood, spirit, and energy is held in these weapons," Zatch said. "The touch of your hands now frees that spirit to enter you!"

Zatch let go. Now the weapons actually were pulsing. Johnny's arms began to vibrate. White light swirled from the weapons, wrapping Johnny in a cocoon of blinding brightness.

Johnny's mouth dropped open. His hair stood on end. He felt his body shake, as if he were being electrocuted.

WHAMM!

In an explosion that filled the entire cave with light, Johnny flew through the air. He landed on the ground, still clutching the weapons.

For a moment he saw and felt nothing. He sat still, not daring to move, not knowing if he was dead or alive.

Slowly his sight returned. Ro-May was there, as were the others. He was alive, all right.

No, he was more than alive. Something had

changed. His body felt different. The weapons were *lighter*, almost as if they were extensions of his own arms.

"Stand and defend yourself!" Zatch barked.

"Huh?" Johnny looked up. Zatch was rushing toward him with a fighting pole.

There was no time to think. Johnny sprang to his feet. The pole whooshed toward him in a deadly arc.

Clank. Johnny blocked the blow with his weapons.

Zatch struck again and again. Each blow was fiercer, sharper.

Johnny's body moved with pure instinct. He blocked and blocked, then began to attack. He knew Zatch was a master. He knew Zatch had defeated Colonel Chi's finest Ninjas with ease. And he knew Zatch was fighting to kill.

But Johnny had been transformed. He had gained a lifetime of Ninja skill and wisdom. And he had lost something, too—a feeling that had paralyzed him only minutes before. Fear.

He fought Zatch to a deadlock. He forced the older man's pole into a position from which he could not pull it. Over the crossed weapons, the two men stared at each other. Their eyes burned with the joy of the fight.

In that moment, Johnny knew that he was ready to face Colonel Chi.

The trail to the Patu San village wound narrowly through the dense jungle. Johnny led the others now. His footsteps were swift and secure, his ears attuned to the slightest sound. He wore his sword in a gilded scabbard around his waist.

Boooooom.

The explosion was muffled and distant. Johnny stopped. Through the trees, he could see a road far down the mountainside. On it was a convoy of trucks and jeeps. Soldiers roamed about, with rifles slung over their shoulders. Near them, a long line of workers stood with picks and shovels. Each worker was chained to the next at the ankle.

"What's that?" Johnny asked Zatch.

Zatch took a pair of binoculars from his pack and peered through them. "It's a chain gang," he said.

"Ah, that's what it is," Johnny said. "I thought it was the world's largest charm bracelet. What are we going to do about it?"

"We have to go around them," Zatch replied. "If we are picked up by one of the patrols, we will wind up prisoners ourselves."

Johnny took the lead again. He found a path around the edge of a steep cliff. In single file, they snaked along slowly—first Johnny, then Adam, Spence, Iggy, Ro-May, and Zatch.

The path became only inches wide. Below them, the cliff dropped straight down. Rivulets of sweat streamed down Iggy's face. "Whoa, this trail's totally narrow," he said nervously. "What if somebody falls?"

Iggy froze. He hadn't meant to say it that way, but—

"AAAAAAAAAAAAAAHHHH!"

The ground broke below Adam. His scream reverberated into the valley below. He reached out desperately, grabbing Spence's arm.

Spence tottered, trying to keep his balance. But Adam had caught him by surprise. Bellowing with fear, he tumbled over the edge.

"Adaaaaaaaammmmm!" Johnny screamed. He and Iggy both reached for Adam. Their feet pushed against the soil, their fingers strained downward.

Then the path crumbled beneath them.

Ro-May and Zatch grabbed them quickly. Johnny and Iggy sprang back onto the ledge.

Their hands were empty. Their eyes were wide with horror.

Below them, Adam's and Lieutenant Spence's screams faded into the valley.

Chapter 15

THE MOUNTAIN WAS STEEP, all right. As steep as any killer wave Adam had ever surfed. It wasn't as smooth, but hey, this was no time to be picky.

He held out his arms for balance. His feet slid down the rock-strewn soil. He managed an excellent Ollie and a gnarly McTwist.

Lieutenant Spence tumbled along beside him, but Adam tried not to look. The old dude had wiped out from the start, and it wasn't a pretty sight.

At the bottom of the mountain they collapsed onto a road. Adam lay there for a while, out of breath and bruised all over. Beside him, Spence was covered with cuts—but he was breathing.

Adam rose to his knees but no farther. Inches from his face was a pair of army boots.

He gulped. Slowly he gazed upward—and found himself staring into the muzzle of a rifle.

A Patu Sani soldier grinned evilly down at him.

"Drop the piece, dirtbag," Lieutenant Spence said. "L.A.P.D. You're under arrest."

The soldier did not answer. With a sudden swing, he smashed Spence's face with the muzzle.

On the narrow ridge, Zatch watched the scene with his binoculars. He saw Spence and Adam rise shakily. He followed them as the soldier led them into a troop transport truck.

With furrowed brow, Zatch lowered the binoculars. "There are too many soldiers. There is nothing we can do for them."

"Hey, that's my brother!" Johnny protested. "I'm going after him."

A smile crept across Zatch's face. He was hearing the voice of a prince now, not a spineless American surf rat.

Johnny perched on the edge and prepared to jump.

"Wait!" Ro-May said, grabbing his arm. "It's too dangerous. You can't do this alone."

"Why do you care?" Johnny retorted. "Are you worried about your precious revolution?"

"No," Ro-May replied, "I'm worried about you."

Johnny met her urgent gaze. She had never looked at him like this before. There was . . . *something* in her eyes. Loyalty, maybe. Even friendship. No, more than that. Johnny felt a warmth in his chest. It spread through his body in an excited shiver of emotion. He smiled. Ro-May cared about him. That much was clear.

He turned back to the cliff, feeling a surge of

strength. Then, without saying a word, he jumped.

Ro-May wasted no time. She jumped right after him.

Iggy watched them in disbelief, then turned to Zatch. "Boy, those kids. They don't weigh the risks, do they? Say, want to grab a cup of coffee?"

Zatch took him by the shoulders and pushed him off the ledge.

Then, after savoring Iggy's screams for a moment, Zatch jumped, too.

They all reached the bottom, bruised but intact. The convoy was now well down the road, and they quietly trekked toward it.

A truck and several jeeps had stopped a half-mile away. Johnny and Ro-May sneaked near them, staying under cover of the dense undergrowth. Iggy and Zatch followed close behind them.

Johnny peered through the branches. Five guards stood around the truck, each armed with assault rifles.

"Stay here," Johnny said, standing up.

Ro-May pulled him down. "No, you wait here."

Before he could say a thing, she drew him into a deep, passionate kiss.

Johnny's head swam. His knees weakened. He didn't want to move. Ever. Forget what had happened at the cave of Kwantzu. Forget the fight with Zatch. Forget everything. It was all *kindergarten* compared to this.

When Ro-May drew away, she looked as dazed as Johnny felt. But she pulled herself together, stood up, and leaped onto the road.

"Hondo gesu geishimasida . . ." she said to the soldiers, with a smile that could have melted Fiberglas.

The soldiers gaped at her in shock. Then broad smiles came across their faces. They started walking toward Ro-May, chuckling under their breath.

It was time for action. Johnny jumped into the soldiers' path. Before they could move a muscle, he became a whirlwind of slashing legs and arms.

With five sharp whacks, Johnny sent the soldiers sprawling to the road.

He and Ro-May shared a smile. But Johnny's job was not done. His brother was in the truck.

Johnny unsheathed his sword. He hopped onto the canvas top and slashed his way through.

Adam and Spence were inside, chained together with the other prisoners. A guard stood over them, looking up in bewilderment.

Landing squarely on his feet, Johnny knocked out the guard with one swift kick. "'Tsup," he greeted his brother.

Adam looked as if Christmas had come early that year. "'Tsup. Did you slide down the mountain?"

"Yeah."

"Wasn't it stylin'?"

"Fully."

Lieutenant Spence raised an eyebrow at Johnny. "Okay, hero, now how are you going to get us out of here?"

Johnny raised the sword of Kwantzu. With a mighty *swoosh,* he brought it down on the chain between Adam and Spence.

The sword struck the metal. Sparks flew. Then, as if they were made of paper, the links simply crumbled away.

The prisoners lifted their arms in wonder. They were free.

"And it's still delicate enough to slice a tomato!" Johnny said.

He began leading the prisoners off the back of the truck. Outside, Ro-May, Zatch, and Iggy joined them.

Johnny shushed them all. Somewhere there were more soldiers. There had to be. He remembered having seen them though the binoculars. Silently he and the prisoners crept along the road, away from the truck. Johnny hoped the soldiers were in the opposite direction, taking a nap or a lunch break.

When he turned a sharp corner, he realized how wrong he was.

The soldiers were waiting. At least forty of them. With at least forty rifles, pointed straight ahead.

"What do you think?" Johnny said to Zatch.

"This is not good," Zatch replied.

"You may only have one eye," Iggy said, "but you don't miss a trick."

Behind them, Adam dropped to his knees. He was surrounded by prisoners, tall ones. He hoped no one would notice his movement.

He began crawling around the prisoners' legs,

back in the direction of the truck and the jeep. He emerged from the back of the crowd, then darted around the corner, out of sight.

He ran to the jeep and looked inside. Keys hung from the ignition. He beamed.

Time to *drive*!

Adam leaped into the driver's seat. He glanced in the rearview mirror. The soldiers were herding all the prisoners back into the truck.

Adam slammed the jeep into reverse. He pulled up alongside the truck and honked the horn.

"Anyone need a ride?"

For a split second, everyone stopped moving. Then the prisoners swung into action. They leaped on their guards, pummeling and kicking.

Johnny jumped into the passenger seat of the jeep. Ro-May, Iggy, Zatch, and Spence all squeezed into the back.

Adam floored the accelerator. The jeep blasted off.

In the rearview mirror, Adam could see some of the guards piling into the other jeeps.

"Hey, seriously," Iggy called from the backseat. "There's some dynamite back here."

"Throw it at them, bro!" Johnny said.

Iggy began lobbing the sticks. The first three bounced off the other jeeps. The fourth bonked one of the drivers on the side of the head. Tires squealing, his jeep swerved into a ditch.

"I got one, I got one!" Iggy crowed.

"Oh, for the love of Kwantzu," Ro-May said. "*Light* them first!"

"I need a light!" Iggy shouted.

With a guilty shift of his eyes, Zatch pulled a pack of cigarettes and a lighter from his pocket. "I really should quit," he said.

"Maybe you should get the Patch," Iggy suggested. Then he slapped himself on the forehead. "Look who I'm talking to."

Lieutenant Spence grabbed the lighter. He began lighting the dynamite and tossing.

Iggy joined him. The Patu Sani jeeps began careening right and left.

BA-ROOOOOOOM! Explosions rocked the ground. The jeeps disappeared behind clouds of gray smoke.

Spence and Iggy stopped throwing. Johnny turned to look. Adam trained his eyes on his mirror.

Then through the cloud came one lone vehicle.

It was a troop truck. But there were no soldiers in sight. A Patu Sani prisoner was driving, and all the others were hanging on the sides.

When they saw Adam's jeep, they burst into wild cheering.

Johnny and Adam whooped with joy.

Adam followed the bumpy road through miles of Patu Sani jungle. In a small clearing they came upon a hut, where a native man waved them to the side of the road.

"He is offering us a meal," Zatch said.

"Chow time!" Johnny called out.

As the family brought out a pot of steaming

food, Zatch reached into his shirt pocket. "Johnny and Adam," he said, "up until now, I did not know if you were worthy. Now I know you are."

"Worthy of what?" Johnny asked.

"This." He held out two headbands, each with the double-headed dragon symbol.

"Kwantzu!" Zatch suddenly shouted, holding the headbands up for all the ex-prisoners to see.

"*KWANTZU!*" roared the Patu Sanis in answer. "*KWANTZU!*"

Zatch tied one of the bands around Johnny's head.

"The headband of a Patu Sani warrior prince," Ro-May said, her eyes filled with admiration.

Adam then leaned forward, and Zatch tied the other band around his head.

"Ahem!" Iggy cleared his throat, hoping Zatch would get a hint. "Ahem!"

When Zatch ignored him, Iggy picked up a stick of dynamite. *"AHEM!"*

"Oh, give him one," Johnny said.

Reluctantly Zatch pulled another band out of his pocket and put it on Iggy.

Johnny smiled at his brother. He hadn't liked the idea of coming to this place, but he could get used to being a prince.

He leaped to his feet and turned toward the troop truck. At the top of his lungs, he yelled, "Kwantzu, dudes!"

With the expectation of happy faces and full stomachs, the ex-prisoners shouted back to their new ruler:

"Kwantzu, dudes!"

Everyone dug into the food. When they all finished, Adam revved the engine and pulled away.

He checked the mirror. The Patu Sani man who lived in the hut was now waving good-bye to his family. As the man climbed into the truck, Adam nodded.

The Patu Sani revolution had its first convert.

Excellent.

Chapter 16

The rebel force grew. In each village Johnny passed, men and women began following behind. They came from the fields, they streamed down the mountainsides. Some brought fighting poles, others grappling hooks and pitchforks. Children threw flowers and rice at the procession.

And all members of the revolution tied on head-bands—headbands that had been hidden away for years, in anticipation of this moment.

By the time they all stopped for a rest, the force had swollen to more than a hundred.

As Johnny knelt by a stream to take a drink of water, Ro-May approached him. "Johnny, can I talk to you for a moment?" she asked.

"Talk to me forever," Johnny said with a grin.

"I've been thinking. I know I talked a lot about marrying you and being queen and every-thing . . ."

"No problem. As soon as we rescue my dad, I'll tell him and—"

"Johnny, all my life I've been doing everything

that was expected of a traditional Patu Sani girl. And . . . well, that was a really swell kiss . . . "

Johnny held out his arms, but Ro-May backed away. "But now," she continued, "well . . . here I am, part of a rebellion . . . "

"And?" Johnny was scared. He didn't like the sound of this.

"And . . . who do my parents think they are, telling me who I'm going to marry? You know? *I'll* decide who I'm going to marry, not them! That is, *if* I marry." Ro-May looked apologetically at Johnny. "I mean, maybe I won't. Maybe I'll go on a career track. Maybe when all this is over I'll go to college, get my master's, and come back and be the first woman prime minister of Patu San."

"Prime minister?"

"Yeah."

Johnny felt as if she had just stabbed him in the heart. "I thought I was supposed to be your king."

"Royalty can be quaint as long as the figurehead monarchs stay out of the way," Ro-May said. "Otherwise, fascist imperialist pigs have a way of being deposed. You know what I mean?"

"Uh . . . yeah," Johnny replied. "Yeah, sure . . . I guess."

"Good. I just didn't want to hurt your feelings about the marriage thing. This whole experience has been such a catharsis."

With a sigh of relief, Ro-May raised a clenched fist and walked away.

Johnny sat there, feeling trashed and burned—

until Ro-May ran back to him. She pulled him toward her and wrapped him in another kiss.

It was as if he had died and gone to heaven, only heaven couldn't possibly feel as good.

As their lips parted, Johnny sank to the ground.

"But we can still date, right?" Ro-May asked.

Johnny nodded. Words would come later, when his mind returned from a short trip to Venus.

The jeep was almost out of gas when they reached a wooded ridge at the end of the road. Over the ridge, the Fortress of Sri Wan was in full view.

The rebels fanned out, lying low. Lieutenant Spence took the binoculars and scanned the entire fortress. "They're expecting an attack," he said. "They've moved some of their guns from the seaward fortress wall so half of them are pointing inland now."

"What about the other side of the island?" Johnny asked.

"There is a reef no ship could get past," Zatch replied. "And with the waves, even a boat with the shallowest draft would run aground."

Ro-May added, "No matter where we attack from, there will be many casualties."

Adam pulled out his Game Gear and turned it on. An image of the fortress appeared. Guns jutted out from the inland and port sides. The north side was undefended.

It was exactly as Spence had described. But that was it. There was no movement, no extra hint of the future.

"It's not showing me anything," Adam said. "I mean, it's supposed to be, like, magic or something, isn't it? I thought it was real."

"The magic *is* real," Zatch insisted, "but it is within you. It always has been. Now, tell me, what do you see?"

Adam looked up from the Game Gear. "Those trees over there."

"Adam, concentrate," Zatch said. "What do you see?"

Squeezing his eyes shut, Adam tried to conjure up magical visions. It was hopeless. "Zatch, I can't do this. All I can see are those trees over there." Suddenly an idea began to form. "What kind of trees are those?"

"Koa," Ro-May replied. "I believe that is what they are called."

Adam kept staring at the trees. They were transforming in his mind—slimming down, flattening, losing their leaves and branches.

In an instant, a forest of sleek surfboards stood before him.

"All *riiiiiiight*," Adam said. He turned to Ro-May. "Are Patu Sanis, like, any good at wood carving and stuff?"

"They are among the best in the world," Ro-May answered.

"Why," Spence said dryly, "you want to buy a souvenir?"

Adam ignored the comment. He was charged now. He knew that if this revolution had any chance, there was work to be done. Lots of work.

That night, in the Dungeon of Sri Wan, Mac lay speechless on the rack. His body screamed with pain, his mind was a muddle of hallucination and reality. But he had not divulged one speck of information to Colonel Chi.

Chi approached him now, carrying an enormous metal helmet. It was shaped like a tiger head, with angry slits for eyes, and a set of knifelike fangs. Manchu followed him with admiring eyes.

"They are out there somewhere," Chi said, practically bristling with excitement, "but when they attack Sri Wan, they will find it a little more difficult than attacking prison guards. Tonight I shall fight with my tiger head!"

He put it over his head. His eyes barely showed through the slits. As he turned to leave, he bumped against the computer console. Then he knocked over a table and a small cart.

He stopped in his tracks. "I think tonight I shall leave my tiger head in the car," came his muffled voice, "where it will strike fear in the hearts of anyone who passes by."

He yanked it off and turned to his assistant. "Manchu, get ready to kill!"

Manchu grinned like a child in an ice cream shop. Giddily he began punching buttons on the computer panel.

The machines of torture creaked into action. And the sound of screaming was music to Manchu's ears.

Chapter 17

OUT OF THE SILVER WATERS rose the sun. The sea birds looked liquid against the waking sky. On the northern beach of Patu San, a silent army gathered on the sand.

Each carried a surfboard carved of koa wood. Each wore the dragon headband of Patu San. Many clutched weapons, ropes, grappling hooks.

Johnny stood at the head of the rebel battalion. It had been a long night, following a long day. Nerves were frayed, fingers were worn to the bone.

Yet the eyes of the Patu Sanis burned with the fire of rebellion. They watched their leader's every move, ready to lay down their lives for his master plan.

Johnny looked out to sea, shading his eyes from the sun.

High tide. The surf was up.

He turned back to his multitude. On the next few moments hung the future of an entire people. Once they started, retreat would be impossible. They would emerge victorious or die in the attempt.

It was now or never. Against the sound of the crashing surf, Johnny cupped his hand to his mouth and shouted, "Let's check out the waves! Kwantzu, dudes!"

The army's roar set the sleeping birds flocking from the trees. *"Kwantzu, dudes!"*

They charged into the water. More than a hundred surfboards slapped downward, more than a hundred pairs of hands plunged in.

Johnny and Adam prepared to join them, but Iggy pulled Johnny back. "Guys," Iggy said, his face pale with fright, "this is going to come as a surprise to you, but—"

"You've never surfed a day in your life," Johnny said.

Iggy looked at him in shock.

"We all know," Adam added. "It's like a big joke."

"Really?" Iggy said.

"Yeah," Johnny replied. "But what if you could surf? It's within you, bro. The ability is within you."

With that, the McQuinn brothers turned and hit the surf.

Iggy watched them intently. "What if I could . . . " he whispered to himself. Gripping his board, he tentatively walked to the water.

The rebels paddled out to the edge of a towering reef. The reef kept them out of sight of the fortress. Once they got around it, they would catch the current into the north shore—provided the ferocious waves didn't destroy them all.

Johnny was the first to catch a wave. Then

Adam. Behind them, the Patu Sani rebels followed as best they could. Some struggled to their feet, others took to the task like serious pound masters.

Call it beginners' luck, call it the spirit of Kwantzu. But somehow they all managed. Even Zatch and Spence.

As for Iggy? Well, he bobbed and jerked. He windmilled his arms. He looked like an infant trying to stand for the first time.

But he had never been happier in his whole life. "I surf!" he screamed at the top of his lungs.

Johnny greeted his troops silently on the shore. The fortress loomed in the distance, its northern side still awaiting the sun.

The rebels ditched their boards. Together they approached the fortress through the sparse brush.

At the base of the fortress wall, they began throwing over their grappling hooks. Then, with the agility of spiders, they climbed upward.

The top of the wall was a wide ledge. A staircase led to the grounds below. The rebels spread out, training their eyes on the scene below.

Masses of troops maneuvered in the stately courtyard. They marched around the shallow, ancient reflecting pools, dragging cannons and artillery. Captain Ming shouted commands, lunging his tiger claw in the air for emphasis. Snipers were already set up, with rifles pointed to the west and south.

Every back was to the northern wall.

Zatch pulled dynamite sticks from his shirt. Lighting each, he passed them to Spence, Johnny, Adam, Ro-May, and Iggy.

At Johnny's signal, they hurled the dynamite downward.

Captain Ming spun around. His eyes bugged out. He shrieked to his men. They swung their rifles toward the rebels.

KAA-BOOOOOOM!

The blast rocked the fortress. Soldiers flew into the air like rag dolls.

"Come on!" Johnny shouted. He ran down the staircase. Screaming, the rebels swarmed behind him.

At the base, Johnny handed Iggy a large *bo* staff. "Here, bro, you're going to need this."

"You mean, we're separating?" Iggy asked.

"Yes!" Johnny retorted. "It's an attack!"

The battle began. Ro-May led a small battalion, kicking and punching. Johnny took on a dozen attackers by himself.

Iggy moved through the fight, trying to concentrate his powers. Around him, the rebels were taking out Chi's soldiers by the dozen. Iggy smiled, proud of himself.

Two soldiers raced toward Spence, their wooden staffs drawn back and ready to strike. Gritting his teeth, Spence ducked. As the staffs flew over his head, he reached upward.

His fingers closed around a staff. He yanked it away and quickly broke it over his knee.

Spence's eyes lit up. It was the same size as an L.A.P.D. nightstick. "Now *this* feels a little more familiar!"

He swung into action, bopping soldiers left and

right. Across the courtyard, Ro-May found herself at the top of a staircase. She glanced down. There seemed to be a million steps, leading downward to a peasant village. Feeling a little dizzy, she looked away.

What she saw made her blood run cold. Manchu was racing toward her with a sword. With a wild flurry of kicks and punches, she sent Manchu flying. Screaming in terror, he tumbled down the endless staircase.

Not far away, Johnny fought off six soldiers at once. He did not see a dark figure emerge from the fortress itself—a dark figure with a half-masked face, a tiger claw, and a gun pointed to Mac McQuinn's head.

Colonel Chi seethed as he watched Johnny fight. He pointed his gun at Johnny and pulled the trigger.

Chapter 18

"JOHNNY!" Mac's voice ripped through the clamor of battle.

Zatch leaped. With reflexes not possible for any but a master of Ninjutsu, he hurled himself into the path of the bullet.

It pierced him in the chest, and he fell to the ground.

With a cry of frustration, Colonel Chi hit Mac over the head with his gun. As Mac slumped to the ground, Chi took aim at Johnny again.

Adam grabbed his Game Gear and threw as hard as he could. It struck Chi's hand, and the gun flew out.

"Yes!" Adam screamed.

"Chi!" Johnny's voice was a growl of anger. He felt no fear of Colonel Chi, only anger and vengeance. For the Patu Sani people. For his step-father.

And for the father and mother he never knew.

Chi met his gaze for one painful moment. Then his eyes darted around the compound. The grounds were littered with the unconscious bodies of his soldiers. Manchu was nowhere in sight.

Without a word Chi turned and ran, disappearing into the tumult.

Groggy, Mac struggled to his feet. He, Johnny, and Adam rushed to the side of their fallen friend. "Zatch!" Johnny cried, cradling him in his arms.

Zatch cringed. Then his eyes flickered closed, and his head lolled to one side.

"Dad, he's not moving!" Johnny yelled.

"Zatch . . . " Adam moaned.

Iggy raced up behind them. His face clouded with horror and sadness.

They all choked back their tears. Zatch was limp and motionless.

Then, slowly, his lips began to move. His barely audible voice rasped, *"What . . . if . . . I . . . don't . . . die?"*

Johnny, Adam, Ro-May, Iggy, and Spence stared in agonized silence. Zatch's eyes began to flutter again. He blinked, then looked up at Iggy. "Hey, it *works!*"

"All *riiiiight!*" Johnny, Adam, and Iggy all yelled.

Zatch struggled to sit up. "Now go," he said, his voice still weak. "You start a battle, you must finish it. Go . . . my nephews . . . " He broke off, wheezing and coughing.

"What did you call us?" Adam asked.

"Nephews," Johnny said. "Why did you call us nephews, Zatch?"

"He is your uncle," Mac replied. "Your father—your *real* father—was the king."

"You're my uncle?" Iggy cried.

"No, not you!" Zatch snapped.

Johnny was stunned. "Why didn't you tell us before?"

"All things have a season," Zatch replied. "It was not time for you to know."

Johnny felt his eyes begin to well up. He and Adam both embraced Zatch.

As Johnny drew back, he said to the others, "You guys gel here with my uncle Zatch. I'm going after Chi."

"You can't go after him alone, kid," Mac said.

Together Adam and Iggy chimed in, "He can if it's his destiny."

Mac let out a deep sigh. "I guess I'll have to listen to you. I'm not going to stop you now."

Unsheathing his sword and trident, Johnny ran in the direction Chi had gone. Mac watched him for a moment. There was no way he was going to sit still. He wanted a piece of Chi himself.

Quickly, quietly, he followed his stepson.

Iggy and Adam helped several rebels hoist Zatch onto a stretcher. "So, Zatch," Iggy said, "you have to tell me, now that this is all over: How did you lose your eye? The whole story, no matter how gruesome."

"I didn't lose it." Zatch lifted his patch halfway, then paused. "Lazy eye. When I talk to people, they don't know which eye to look at. It's really embarrassing."

"Really?" Iggy said.

Zatch let the patch snap back into place. "Rank!"

Johnny wound his way through the courtyard. Chi's soldiers swarmed toward him, swords slashing. They backed him to the top of the long staircase. Johnny fought back, wielding the sword of Kwantzu with blinding speed.

Below him, Manchu slowly climbed toward the top of the stairs. His hulking body was covered with cuts and bruises from his fall. As Johnny came into view, he smiled.

Manchu sprinted up the last few steps. With a grunt of agony and triumph, he grabbed Johnny from behind.

Thud. Manchu hadn't seen Mac to his left—but he sure felt the whack on his head. He roared with pain and let go of Johnny.

Johnny landed on his feet and whirled around. With a strength he'd never thought he had, he lifted Manchu over his head and spun him around.

Then, at the very top of the stairs, Johnny let go. "Who-o-o-oa!" Manchu's scream faded into the distance as he tumbled downward, head over heels.

Johnny watched—until he heard a thunderous crash behind him.

A low cement wall exploded into dust as a jeep smashed through. It sped toward Johnny, its tires squealing. Behind the wheel was Colonel Chi.

Johnny jumped away. Chi yanked the steering wheel toward him. The jeep's tires left the ground.

He barreled toward Johnny again, this time firing a handgun.

With lightning moves, Johnny used the sword of Kwantzu to bat the bullets away—right back to the jeep.

Pow! Pow! Pow! Pow! The jeep's tires exploded.

SKREEEEEEEE! The jeep skidded into a wall. Its hood blew open.

A gusher of water spewed from the radiator. It arched upward, then drizzled down onto Chi.

"Agggh! I'm wet!" Chi shrieked, holding up his claw in horror.

But the claw remained still. Chi smiled. "I'm okay!"

He jumped out of the jeep. Reaching into the backseat, he pulled out a machine gun.

Johnny knew even the sword of Kwantzu wouldn't protect him from that. He turned and ran.

But Adam was nearby, and he had some ideas of his own. He trained his Game Gear on Chi. Immediately an image of Chi and Johnny appeared on the screen. Frantically Adam moved the controls.

Dzzzzzzzt. Chi's claw began to lurch, spitting electrical sparks. It threw the machine gun to the ground.

Johnny turned and unsheathed his sword. His eyes burned with vengeance. As he stepped forward, Chi backed up a short stairway, onto a ledge that surrounded the fortress.

Chi gulped. "Uh . . . you have a sword, and I'm without my gun. Don't you want this to be a fair fight?"

Johnny knew he was right. To kill Colonel Chi with the sword of Kwantzu would be too easy. Better to face him on equal terms.

He opened his fingers. The sword dropped to the ledge, then fell to the ground.

Chi lunged. He clamped his tiger claw around Johnny's throat.

Johnny tried to pull the claw off, but it was too tight. He staggered backward, gagging.

Adam punched the controls of his Game Gear. Sparks began to fly from Chi's wrist. The claw twitched and flexed. It let go of Johnny's throat, then went for Chi's.

"No!" Chi cried. But this time he was helpless.

And Adam was not about to let him go.

Chi stumbled backward along the ledge. Under him, the reflecting pool was bright with the rising sun.

The claw clutched Chi's throat and pushed. Chi dug his heels in, trying desperately to get his bearings.

"YEAAAAAAHHHHH!" Johnny let out a triumphant scream and leaped. He rose from the ledge, leg muscles coiled and ready to strike.

Chi struggled below him, white with fear. One swift kick would do him in, no sweat.

No, Johnny thought. Ninjutsu was not necessary. He landed on two feet, inches from Chi.

Chi yanked his claw from his throat. A grin formed on his face. He laughed at Johnny—mocking him, *daring* him.

Johnny raised one finger. He touched it gently to Chi's forehead and pushed.

Chi's heels were at the edge of the ledge. He lost his balance. He windmilled his arms in

Then, with a bloodcurdling scream, Chi fell off the ledge. He landed in the pool with a splash.

The last Johnny—or anyone—ever saw of Colonel Chi was a bright display of electric sparks bubbling out of the reflecting moat.

Johnny sank to his knees with exhaustion. The revolution was over.

Chapter 19

THE ROYAL WELCOMING CEREMONY was set up for the next day. Thousands of Patu Sani faithful showed up at the palace. The two thrones of the crown princes, hidden away for years by the hopeful villagers, were polished and set on a platform for all to see.

To the blaring of traditional ram horns, Ro-May led Johnny and Adam up the red carpet to their rightful places.

Iggy stood on the platform among the other dignitaries. He leaned down to whisper to a nearby child, "They're just the decoys, see? I'm the king, you're my subjects, and she's my chick. Enjoy!"

On the platform, Ro-May took Johnny and Adam around for introductions. First was a sage-looking gray-bearded man. "Your Highnesses," she said, "may I present a great holy man who was born in your father's native village—the Baba-Ram of Mee Grob."

Johnny's eyes widened. The Baba-Ram began to bow, then stopped. "Wait a second," he said, staring at Johnny. "I know this guy. This is a funny guy. I *love* this guy. He knocks me out! 'Barbara Ann.' Funny stuff!"

Johnny smiled and bowed. Ro-May then led him and Adam to the thrones. Behind them stood Iggy, Mac, Spence, and Zatch.

As the new crown princes turned to sit, the crowd hushed.

"I think they're waiting for you to say something," Ro-May whispered.

Johnny gave Adam and Iggy a helpless look. "I've got nothing."

"Maybe this will inspire you," Ro-May said, giving him the hottest kiss this side of the South China Sea.

"Bro, I'll handle it," Johnny said with renewed confidence. He stood up and shouted to his countrypeople, "Kwantzu, dudes!"

The crowd began to chant with delirious happiness: *"Kwantzu, dude! Kwantzu, dude! Kwantzu, dude . . . "*

Johnny held out his hands, palms down. "Gel out! Gel, my people, gel!" All night long he'd been thinking about what to do as king, and he'd reached some conclusions. They might not be what the people expected, but hey, they had no choice. He had to do what was right. For him and Ro-May.

As they quieted down, he announced, "As my first act as your king, I hereby dissolve the monarchy and give the government back to the people—because it is your destiny to be free!"

Out of the corner of his eye, Johnny spotted Manchu climbing to the top of the long staircase.

His eyes were glazed, his body slumped and battered. Clenching his fists, Manchu lurched toward Johnny.

With a swift kick, Johnny sent him flying. Manchu landed at the top of the long staircase and began another free fall.

Clearing his throat, Johnny continued. "And so, my people, as my future queen and I go off to take our SATs, please remember that we are all created equal. And just because I was born into royalty, I am no different from you. Now put my face on a stamp and we'll call it a day."

The Patu Sanis let out a roar of approval.

"And for now," Johnny yelled, "later, my people!"

To a swelling chorus of cheers, Johnny, Adam, and Iggy were hoisted onto chairs and lifted high into the air.

For the rest of that glorious day, they rode on the shoulders of the people through the streets of Patu San.

It wasn't surfing, but it was easily as cool.

Circumstances were left different. The weapons were faster, stronger, as if they were expressions of his own anger.